The Left Palm

and
Other Halloween Tales of the Supernatural

By Evelyn Klebert

The Left Palm
And Other Halloween Tales of the Supernatural
By Evelyn Klebert

A Cornerstone Book
Published by Cornerstone Book Publishers

Interior Photographs by Evelyn Klebert

First Cornerstone Edition - 2009
Second Cornerstone Edition - 2019
Third Cornerstone Edition - 2024

Cornerstone Book Publishers
Hot Springs Village, AR
www.cornerstonepublishers.com

ISBN: 978-1-93493-556-9

For all of those who are enchanted

by the season

Table of Contents

The Left Palm

and
Other Halloween Tales of the Supernatural

Wolves

"Wolves." His eyes widened from behind the rather well-worn spectacles he wore precariously perched on the edge of his nose. He wasn't a young man, but in contrast, a wiry, elderly fellow who didn't much like change and even less, surprises. So, in a procrastinating fashion, he removed the glasses, pulled out an old handkerchief from his back pocket, and leisurely wiped the lenses while his still razor-sharp mind contemplated a backdoor out of this dilemma. He grumbled, again positioning the glasses on the end of his nose and giving just the hint of a smile that said he was just an old fool — an old fool running a curio shop in the French Quarter. Taking a deep breath that felt clearly as though it rattled somewhere in the recesses of his brittle ribs, he played his best cards. "Is there something in particular I could help you with today?"

There was the finest flicker of a smile across a pair of young, dark red lips. The eyes in a fine-boned oval face stared back at him as though they were neatly and concisely ripping away the layers of his well-contrived façade. The eyes were green. His wife, Roberta, of nearly sixty years, had green eyes as well, but not at all like these. His wife's eyes were filled with light and color. But not these. These were dark, like a forest on the verge of night. Any light that tried to reflect was muffled out by something unseen within.

The mouth was moving, and he was watching it curiously, compelled perhaps, he thought somewhat distantly. Was she trying to entrance him or suffocate him? At this moment, both felt like a tangible probability.

"Wolves," she murmured again. Of course, he knew of what she was speaking. He might play the fool from time to time, but he certainly wasn't one. Long ago, he was told when it was first placed in his keeping that someone would come for it one day with only that single word as their calling card. And he, out of more than obligation — out of a binding indisputable agreement — must surrender it. Of course, at the time, he was well-paid. In fact, he had never been better paid for any single acquisition in all his years. But it was so long ago, thirty, perhaps closer to forty years back. And that payment was just a distant, fleeting memory now. While the object itself, well, it was worth an untold fortune.

Abruptly interrupting the meandering of his mind, he felt a slim hand come to rest on his. His eyes looked down. They were long, slender fingers, flesh more pale than warmed by the sun. But then, the delicate hand began to squeeze with a strength he did not understand. "I don't have time for this old man. Give it to me," she rasped. Those lightless eyes were wide now and so very frightening.

"Give you what?" He choked out. But it was his final lie. For in his mind, as clear as though he was seeing it before him, his building, his store of so many years, and him within were engulfed in flames. It must be happening now, in the moment, for the flames were wildly everywhere, burning him, scorching his flesh on his arms, until he could see the white of his very own skeleton. "Uoohh" he gasped, the unintelligible and desperate words of a dying man.

And then clearly, sharply penetrating into the horror of his own hell, he heard a voice — a voice speaking to him within his mind. "Now let's try this again," she whispered because there was no need to shout. She had won. "Wolves," this time, it rolled off her tongue like the sweetest poetry.

"This is foolishness, pure foolishness, my dear."

She grimaced, "So you've said." She perched the cell phone unstably on her shoulder and checked the rear-view mirror. What was foolish was taking a call on an unfamiliar highway while she was driving an unfamiliar rental car.

"Where are you now?"

"I'm driving." Luckily, it was a clear stretch, this last piece of the journey between New Orleans and the small south-central city. That was her destination.

"You're not going to tell me, are you?"

"It's best not. I'll fill you in when everything is done."

"And you, my little sister, will you be done too?"

She frowned. How she loved her older brother, his protectiveness. Ostensibly, he was the only family she had, except for certain unknown factions. But just now, his protectiveness felt more than a bit smothering. "Well, let's hope not."

"Are you sure you're reading that thing right? What if you end up with the wrong one?"

"Charles, you have to have a little faith. I am not without my own gifts."

"Cecile, I don't want to lose you."

"I know. Just have a little trust in me."

On the way into town, she picked up a street map so she wouldn't be entirely clueless as to where she was going. And then, just off the highway, she checked into a motel. It was one of a moderately priced chain. She'd stayed in better. She could most certainly afford better. She and her brother had money. Her parents had left them well off when they died. But just now, the surroundings didn't matter much. She only needed a place to regroup.

Cecile placed her small suitcase on the bed and sat quietly beside it, contemplative. What she'd done to the old man in the antique shop had been cruel and unfair. And certainly, on some level, she was ashamed. But she'd sensed his greed, his reluctance to relinquish it, the thing she needed.

Steadying her nerves, she reached into her black leather purse and drew out the bundle of material she'd wrapped it in. It was a fine white, raw silk piece of fabric. Rather gingerly, she laid it on the bed and began to unwrap its folds. Already, her fingertips quivered from the emanations of power, although she had not even touched it. It sat there in its own mahogany box latched with a clasp of pure silver. It was quite valuable, perhaps priceless in its construction — certainly in its origin. It was understandable that the old man did not want to part with it.

She rubbed the palms of her hands together briskly, trying to drive away the chill that had settled into her fingers. She had spent enough years studying the magical arts to know that handling such powerfully enchanted tools did come with a price. Taking a nearly painful breath, she quickly flipped the latch, opening the box of the Houdin Trouveur.

That it was stunning was undeniable — beautiful, quite ornate, constructed purely of platinum and black onyx. The platinum arms of the antiquated compass fluttered for a moment and then swirled in a deliberate direction, markedly toward the southeast. He would be there. The murderer of her parents was somewhere in this city.

Something was off. He'd felt it all day, deep down in his skin, actually the night before as well. And irritatingly, the dreams had come, a sweep of redness and then fire, fire exploding pure and white. What it all meant, he wasn't so sure. He'd given up this divination business, this reading of dreams, some time ago — in fact, two hundred years ago, to be exact. For some time, with the exception of a few minor lapses, life had become quite placid for Ethan Garraint. That was the name he'd adopted several decades earlier. And, he had to admit, he'd grown fond of it. This part of the country was quite welcoming to those of a French descent, and he'd been born nearly five hundred years before in a small province near modern day Avignon.

Ethan continued to polish a heavy, black oak wardrobe mirror that he'd just put the finishing touches on for the festival today. He enjoyed working with black oak. There was something depthless about its sheen. But then again, black oak, pine, maple, and cherry wood all had their respective charms. For a moment, he glanced at the reflection serenely staring back at him from the long oval mirror. From his appearance, he could not be mistaken for a man of more than thirty. His light blue-grey eyes and thick blonde hair suggested an almost innocent quality that his soul did not agree with. He'd been alive too long and seen too much to be naïve about much of anything.

He finished polishing the wood of the mirror, more interested in his creation than anything else. He'd found some solace through the long years and endless solitude in developing this craft. There was a strange contentment he'd found in working with the wood. It eased the burdens that his unusual life had deemed he should carry. In some ways, he felt as though, in his work, he imbued his creations with small pieces of his soul. After all, even he couldn't live forever. Not with so many people trying to kill him.

"How will you be able to find him with it? Doesn't it just seek out any werewolf?" Charles had asked her this, among other questions, before she'd set out from Boston nearly five days ago.

"Well, I haven't spent all these years studying and developing my own gifts without the intent of making use of them. I will work an incantation that will affix the Houdin Trouveur solely toward him, toward our parent's killer."

He'd stared at her with a great deal of anxiety in his acute, dark eyes. "I don't like it. And regardless of your intentions, I don't think our parents would like it either."

She frowned explicitly, "Well, they're not here to give us an opinion, are they?"

He looked away, clearly disturbed by her words. "I know they would want you to get on with your life, Cecile, not become obsessed with vengeance."

They had this discussion before countless times. But evidently, Charles felt it worthwhile to try one last attempt to dissuade her. "They weren't the type to look the other way. They wouldn't have allowed an injustice to stand. You knew them. You were older when they died."

His eyes flickered gently across her face. He was a strong man, a stern man, except when it came to his younger sister. He had always reserved his kinder nature for his dealings with her. "They had limits Cecile. They were human. I know they wouldn't have approved of how deeply you've gone into these dark arts."

She hardened herself. Now was not the time to be thrown off course — not when she was so close. "I've only done what was necessary. I can't go after Le Guerrier unprotected."

He smiled grimly, "Don't call him that. It makes him sound too much like a myth. No, I know that you feel you've done what you've had to. But at what cost Cecile?"

She blocked his words from her mind. She couldn't afford to question herself now, not now. "It's time Charles. Did you get me what I need?"

"Yes," he said quietly, seemingly resigned for the moment. "The location of the seeker."

She'd smiled broadly. If he was nothing else, Charles Bissett was thorough. "And the password to get it?"

"Yes, my dear one, all of that, but finding the monster won't kill him for you."

She so wished he was not so anxious. If anyone should be, it should be her. But an odd sort of serenity had settled within her. Perhaps, it was the acknowledgment of what she must do, her acceptance of what her long years of aimlessness and restlessness had brought her to. "I know that. I've spent years tracking Le Guerrier. I've researched, learned every scrap, every nuance that is knowable about him."

"But these last fifteen years he's completely fallen off the radar. Even with my extensive connections, no one knows anything. How do you even know he's alive?"

"I know it." She stated flatly with complete conviction. "I would know if he were dead."

He straightened up in the brown leather chair by the fireplace in their study. In that moment, it struck her quite poignantly. She remembered all of the nights that she'd curled up in it as a little girl when her nightmares kept her from sleep. In a fleeting twist of yearning, she wondered if she would ever see it or her brother again. "How would you know it, Cecile?" he asked.

A simple question with such a complicated answer, "Because I would feel peace if he were dead." There was a look in his eyes at this — perhaps sadness, perhaps disbelief. "Don't worry, Charles," she murmured.

"I can't help it. I don't want to lose you too."

"I can beat him. I know him completely."

And then he smiled grimly, "But what if he's changed?"

She'd packed the tiny pistol deep within her purse. It was loaded with three silver bullets that Charles had managed to get blessed by a Bishop in Northern Massachusetts. Anyone else making such a request would probably have been tossed out unceremoniously on their backside, but not Charles. Charles was a rich man, and money and donations often made the ridiculous become acceptable.

Late the previous night, Cecile had performed an intricate locator spell on the Houdin Trouveur. It had enabled her to gain a more precise fix on his location. But as a consequence, it had drained her terribly. The magical compass had to pull in a great deal of energy from its user to fulfill its purpose. She hadn't anticipated the severity of this complication. It was clear she should use the Trouveur as seldom as possible lest she lose too much of her own power. She slept deeply that night and dreamed of crowds of people laughing and dancing and colorful booths and exhibits all about her. Then she saw fire, white blinding fire, somewhere else.

When she ventured into the lobby that morning for coffee, she noticed the signs hanging up promoting the festival. It was then that she made the connection. Clearly, these were the images from the night before. Donning blue jeans, a white cotton shirt, a pair of lace-up, and black leather boots she'd bought on a trip to France the year before, Cecile then obtained directions to the festivities. Oddly enough, it turned out to be precisely southeast of her location. Everything was falling into place, and that, more than anything, made her extremely uneasy.

Amelia Gerard had just turned twenty and majored in communications at the local university. As the crowds milled around her on this bright Saturday in October, she felt annoyed and somewhat preoccupied. She'd left behind a group of friends near the stage, listening to one of the musical acts booked for the festival. She'd told them she was going for another beer. Instead, she bypassed the refreshment stands and wandered most deliberately into the artisan section.

Although there was quite a mixing of people and more than a little stirring of dust from the ground, she could locate the man she sought quite readily. She stood to the side of the booth where he'd set up his collection of furniture pieces for the occasion. She waited quietly, but not entirely patiently, as he finished talking to what she surmised was a potential customer. It was some minutes before he noticed her, but he did greet her with a welcoming smile that, at that moment, felt well worth the wait. "Ms. Gerard."

"Mr. Garraint," she responded lightly.

He wore a dark t-shirt with khaki pants that she thought made him look particularly handsome, but then again, she was completely smitten with the man. "So, are you enjoying the festival on this fine day?" He asked with his fluid drawl that she had never quite been able to identify. It wasn't exactly local, but in some ways, it did seem a bit French.

She tipped her head a bit, warming under his gaze, "Well, it's a bit crowded and a bit loud. But other than that, I'd have to say yes."

He moved a rocking chair he'd been showing to someone further back into the open booth as he spoke to her. It felt odd to think she'd met him only a few months earlier. Then, she'd been involved in a project for a journalism class, interviewing local artists.

Initially, perhaps due to her ignorance, she hadn't considered furniture making an art. But once she met Ethan Garraint, she was enlightened, and that opinion was radically revised. Intriguing indeed seemed too ineffectual a word to describe him. There was an aura about him, a subtle but powerfully enigmatic aura that captivated her. She was quite sure he was a good ten years her senior, but that hadn't stopped her from forming a romantic interest. After all, she always considered herself quite mature for her age.

He nodded, "It is busy today. But that's good for everyone's business." His eyes flickered over her only briefly, and then he continued to glance around the crowds as though he was watching for something.

"Is everything all right, Ethan?" She asked, wondering why she was not holding his attention today.

He glanced up at her, looking a bit pensive, then smiling. "You should go find your friends, Amelia, and enjoy yourself. I'm afraid I'll be quite busy with things here today."

Her eyes widened, and then he nodded, reaffirming his previous declaration. She was being dismissed, and it chaffed, particularly his abruptness. But she did have to admit, there was something else in his voice that was quite grave, that told her this was for her own good. Although why, she couldn't quite put her finger on. "All right then, have a good day." She murmured reluctantly.

"Yes, yes, and you as well."

From some yards away, Cecile watched. It must be him, but she couldn't be positive. And she certainly couldn't confront him in the middle of such a crowd. Werewolf or not, she would be arrested for shooting an unarmed man. The only way to be positive was to use the Trouveur. But that, too, was risky. It was too powerful to go unnoticed by such an ancient magical being. In addition, it would tip her hand and, in all probability, leave her to the same fate as her parents.

Her eyes locked on and carefully followed the young blond he'd been speaking to.

With great focus, she sent out an impulse that encouraged her to pass near Cecile. As she did, Cecile propelled a discreet energy marker toward her that landed on the woman's arm. With this in place, she could be easily traced when Cecile had need of her.

Amelia left the fairgrounds around five. Her friends intended to stay much later and move on to some downtown clubs as the evening progressed, but she had been seized by a strange fatigue and melancholy. She knew she was being silly. There was nothing between her and Ethan Garraint, nothing but her own fantasies. The man had always been kind, cordial, and charming in a way that some might construe as flirtatious, but then again, it could just be his manner.

She flung open the door to her dorm room, shutting it loudly behind her, and flopping vigorously onto the bed. If she was anything, she was practical and knew when to cut her losses. Tomorrow, she would remove Mr. Garraint from her consciousness and her radar. Then, she would look around to find other, more attainable fish in the sea. She closed her eyes, letting the excessive tiredness she felt take hold. It could have been moments, or even hours later, when she awoke to the sound of a very quiet knock on her door. Amelia glanced at the clock by her bed. It was six-thirty. Sara, her roommate, wasn't due back for some time yet.

Slowly sitting up, she was feeling a bit disoriented. But again, merely seconds later, there was another light tap on the door. "Just a minute," she called out, her voice still croaky from sleep.

She rose on shaky feet, trying to smooth out her long blond hair as she approached the door. She wondered distractedly if she was getting sick because the room actually felt as though it was swirling around her. Her trembling hand touched the knob. It felt cold and moist beneath her fingertips. But then maybe it was her. Her hands did feel strangely clammy right now.

Just before she turned the knob, it occurred to her, like a flash through her mind, that she shouldn't. But her pragmatic sense pushed that impulse aside as she opened the door. In that instant, time seemed to rush around her in a blur as an impossibly strong hand reached out and grabbed her by the throat.

Ethan began to close up his booth somewhere around seven in the evening. Others set up near him had left earlier, but he waited as long as he could. He was expecting something. He was no clairvoyant, but he did have very acute feelings and a sense of things. Today, he sensed a menace about. And more to the point, he smelled it. There was dark magic in the air.

So, he waited and watched all day. But this menace was a clever one and remained hidden. This, however, did not overly concern him. One thing he did have that all these extraordinarily young souls milling about him seemed to lack was patience — infinite, inexhaustible patience. He could wait it out.

As he loaded his small van with the pieces of furniture that did not sell at the fair, he heard footsteps approaching the truck from quite a distance. His powerful sense of smell identified their author rather quickly. He smiled to himself even before she reached him.

Persistent was a word that seemed appropriate.

He allowed her to approach without turning around as he finished packing the van. This type of complication he felt quite sure he could manage with very little peril to himself.

"Ethan," she whispered.

And then, he turned around with a smile. "Amelia, this is a very isolated place for you to be alone."

She did not smile back at him in her usual, coquettish manner. "I'm not alone. You're here. Aren't you concerned about it being so isolated?"

He eyed her with curiosity. She was in a serious mood tonight, not her ordinarily light-hearted self. "I am not a young, beautiful woman, and I can handle myself." He frowned, "What's the matter, little one? You seem very grim tonight."

She tilted her head a bit, and those lovely blue eyes looked at him oddly in the semi-darkness. "I need to talk to you, Ethan, about something very serious. Can we go somewhere private?"

He grinned a bit, trying to put her more at ease. "Now, that might ruin your reputation."

But he was a bit surprised. It did nothing to thaw the gravity of her demeanor. "It's important, please."

"I was headed back to the store to bring the furniture."

"Could we go there and talk?" Her voice sounded nearly pleading, but it didn't reach the eyes. They remained distant. Something was definitely amiss. It seemed clear to him now that it was best to discover what all this was about.

"Where is your car?"

She shook her head, soft blond hair whipping about her shoulders. "A friend dropped me."

He nodded, "Fine, then let's go."

She said nothing but quietly climbed into the van's front seat beside him.

It becomes quite odd when a scenario you've built up in your mind since literally, you were a child, finally comes to fruition. Every nuance is painstakingly planned, pulled somewhere from an endless well of grief, then later disappointment, and nursed to an excruciatingly fine point of razor-sharp detail.

She had rehearsed the scene all her life. She had put endless preparations into the part and lived and breathed for just these few paltry moments. And nothing, absolutely nothing, was as she expected.

Cecile retreated into some quiet place, where the observer watched and marveled at the contradictions that reality unravels. The man next to her was charming and warm. He was not the cold and brittle like the killer of her dreams, but something else entirely. As they walked into the dimly lit front room of his St. Julien Street establishment, his calm, soothing demeanor sickened her. It twisted at her like a poorly placed knife, lodged somewhere precariously between her ribs, making breathing a bit difficult.

As she crossed the threshold, a sudden blurriness swept up in front of her eyes. She forced her mind to concentrate and funnel even more energy into her façade, although she knew it was ill-advised. Taking on the form of another visage was a gamble, risky, stretching well beyond her own limitations. It couldn't go on for long. Besides, it was best to finish him off before he was onto her — best to be done with it. But the idea of just killing him now and leaving felt oddly empty. She needed more to put this all at rest. She needed—

He grabbed her arm to steady her. "Are you all right, Amelia?"

She nodded and murmured. "Yes, just feeling a little weak. I haven't eaten." She tried to avoid his eyes. She had read an account once from a seventeenth-century monk chronicling the history of Northern Gaul. It was a local uprising, in some obscure way involving Le Guerrir. The monk referred quite pointedly to the hypnotic quality of the foreigner's eyes. She remembered it now, thinking it strange at the time. After all, wasn't it vampires, not werewolves, who held the hypnotic gaze? Then again, he had lived an abnormally long time and had no doubt picked up a few interesting tricks along the way.

She felt his hand gently grasp her chin, deliberately tilting her head up to face him. She had no choice. Her pistol was in her purse, which was not exactly accessible right at that moment. She allowed her gaze to meet his, concentrating heavily on the incantation that separated her from disaster.

The light was dim, but his eyes were markedly darker than she remembered at the festival grounds. They were blue but also a gray — not a light grey but a dark, turbulent one. He was looking for something. He felt the difference. She was sure of it but hopefully hadn't fleshed it out yet. "Tell me. What's really wrong?" he murmured.

Her heart was beating wildly with fear. She dug, dug deep into the flashes she'd picked up out of Amelia Gerard's mind, even as she ravaged and drained her life's energy earlier this evening. Then, she hadn't thought about how ruthless she'd been, and now there was no time to reflect on such collateral damage. Desperate, she hooked onto something — her unrequited affection for this man. It was just enough to throw him temporarily off-balance. With deliberation, she put her arms around his neck, reaching up and giving him the most passionate kiss she could muster.

At first, she felt him freeze in total surprise. Good, that's exactly what she wanted. Keep him surprised and off-balance. And then, in a startling movement, he pulled her closer and returned the kiss with a fervor she found completely unexpected. She expected a rejection, not capitulation.

In reflex, forgetting where she was and what she was doing, Cecile abruptly tore herself out of the embrace. "What are you doing?" she spat out without thinking.

He stood there, staring at her, and then his face broke out in a smile that she could only describe as quite engaging. "I was kissing you back, my dear. You know, you really should decide what you want."

She quickly regrouped, returning with the most insipid, vulnerable expression she could concoct. "I want you to stop toying with me, Ethan. I want to mean something to you, not be a passing fancy."

The smile drifted away from his mouth, and a grimmer expression replaced it. "Perhaps we should talk this out, Amelia." He motioned to a small cherry wood dinette at the back of the shop. "Why don't you sit down, and I'll make us a cup of tea." She nodded, still trying to look the part of a confused, lovesick female. She clutched her purse close to her side and slowly sat at the table.

Softly, he patted her back and whispered, "Be back in just a minute." And then he disappeared into a back room. She looked down. Her eyes were blurring again. Twenty minutes to half an hour was the very longest she could retain the appearance of Amelia Gerard. Her hand reached down into her purse and fingered the pistol, but the back of it brushed against the cloth that held the Trouveur. Even through the material, it burned against her hand.

She was sure it was him. It must be. But she would like to confirm it before she took his life. This much she owed to her parents, to be absolutely sure. She grasped the Trouveur and placed it on the table.

He had a small kitchen in one of the back rooms of his shop. It was a galley across from which was the larger studio where he did much of his woodwork. There was an old-fashioned kettle that he was using to heat up the water for their tea. Of course, the microwave would be much faster, but he wanted to take the extra minutes to contemplate. It seemed as though all the hairs on the back of his neck were standing on end, alerted, in nearly a violent fashion, to a danger in his proximity.

But all that was present was Amelia — beautiful, unpredictable, and dare he say unstable Amelia. He placed the teabags into the two mugs as the copper kettle rattled on the stove. He enjoyed the simplicity of his life these days, minus all the trappings that people often become so intertwined with.

He took the kettle off the stove, poured the steaming water into the cups, and watched quietly as they steeped. In a life stripped of those things that separate one from clear vision, it is easier to discriminate truth from illusions.

The things he'd felt essentially about Amelia were oddly distorted tonight. She was not a person to behave erratically. She was conservative and practical and would not gamble unless it was warranted. But tonight, he swirled one of the tea bags in the hot water until it bled its color throughout, did not add up. He didn't smell alcohol. He didn't detect drug use, and for her, that, too, would have been completely out of character.

He turned toward the front room, reacting to something subtle—a sort of crackle in the air. And then suddenly, directly in his heart area, he felt a pressure so acute that he flinched at its impact.

What he did next was foolish, but he had come to live a simple, uncomplicated life as much out of the shadows as was possible for a creature like him. So, he walked, without caution, quickly into the front room.

The table, where he'd left her, was unoccupied. But even from where he stood, he could see a nearly luminescent object sitting on top of it. The gentle pressure in his heart only intensified as he approached, but nothing could quell his curiosity. It was perhaps a yard away from it that he stopped. His curiosity was quite satisfied, as he clearly identified what he was looking at. One piece to an irritating puzzle had fallen in place. "That bastard Houdin," he muttered with part contempt and part amusement. "He swore he'd destroyed the damn thing."

And then, from behind a large cypress armoire, a rather shadowy figure emerged. Her voice was not mellow and fluid like Amelia's but instead deep and raspy. "Too bad for you that he didn't."

His eyes first took in the tiny pistol pointed at him and second the features of the woman that held it. The hair was long, thick, and auburn, and the eyes, as far as he could perceive, a dark mossy green shade. At this, the rest of the puzzle fell into place, for the resemblance was unmistakable. He smiled broadly, never one to face his own demise without a light heart. "Well, if I'm not mistaken, you must be Cecile. I've made it my business to keep track of the Bissett children." She frowned. Evidently, that wasn't the reaction she'd been expecting. "I knew your mother. She was a resourceful woman but evidently not as resourceful as you are."

Her voice was quiet and steely, "I'm here to kill you."

He nodded, "So I see, but not before we have a nice visit, I hope. After all, I'm the only one who can tell you the truth about your parents' death."

The noise in her head roared around her in the room, but it was clear that he didn't hear it. She steadied herself, although her knees shook with weakness. With extreme concentration, she gripped the pistol, although her hands were so chilled she could scarcely feel herself holding it.

She could see Charles in her mind as clearly as if he stood before her. "At what cost, Cecile? Revenge at what cost?"

Her vision was blotchy, and parts of the room were completely blotted out. When she'd used the Trouveur this time, it had been different. It glowed and shook, and then the pointer spun in the direction of the back room. But before it was finished, she'd felt it emanate something, a force that had been subtle before. It pulled energy from her, tearing it directly out of her heart. But she couldn't let him see. She only had to finish it. That was all that mattered.

"I'm not a fool Le Guerrir. Do you really think I've come here for a chat?"

He moved slightly, but she wasn't sure. Her vision was so bad now. Everything was indistinct light and shadows. "Your mother was a very determined woman. I think finishing me off might have been a feather in her cap. But your father, I don't think he cared much, except for her. She was everything to him."

He'd moved now. She was sure. "Stay still, or I'll end all of this now."

The movement stopped. The only way she could see him was reflected in light. Was this what it was like going blind? She followed the impressions that were left in her vision. "It was in Italy, you know. I don't like to travel much now, but I did that year. They didn't know it, but I came there to learn from a master furniture maker. Isn't that amusing? The werewolf hunted down because he wanted to make furniture better?"

She breathed deeply, raggedly. She could see her parents in her mind, and then Charles and then Amelia. She'd left her on the floor of her dorm room, not dead, but close to it. "Stop talking," she rasped.

"You know, they thought it would be safe that night. It wasn't a full moon. It would be an easy kill for them. They thought. But the wolf came out that night."

There were deep, ravaging, painful breaths now. "What do you mean?"

She looked around the room, but she'd lost sight of him. He wasn't moving, just hidden in the shadows. "I learned how to summon the wolf without the necessity of a full moon. An old magician taught me." She focused on the direction of his voice, but it seemed to be coming from everywhere. "His name was Houdin."

It seemed moments before the reality rolled over her. "What, what did you say?"

"A 19th-century magician, cantankerous fellow, but loyal and brilliant. Haven't you figured it out yet, Cecile?"

"What?" she murmured. She couldn't feel her hands at all. They were like ice, as was her skin, as was her mind.

"That thing, the Trouveur that you've been using, has been killing you, feeding a poisonous fire into your veins."

"That's impossible," she barely was able to get the words out. He was standing next to her, but she couldn't stop him. She couldn't feel the gun. It might have dropped. She didn't know.

"The Trouveur kills the person who uses it. Slowly, I grant you, but my friend was a merciless bastard."

She slipped down to her knees, seeing Charles taking her out of the chair in the study when she was a little girl, whispering away the nightmares. She barely heard his voice. "He was merciless, but I am not." She heard the low growl beside her but did not see the wolf. She'd already walked into the white fire.

Two days later, Amelia Gerard woke up in the hospital. Her mother was sitting beside her, holding her hand. Tears were running down her face as Amelia first opened her eyes. Two days after that an arrangement of yellow roses arrived with a card that read, *Best Wishes on a Speedy Recovery, All My Regards, Ethan.* That was the last time she ever heard from him.

Emma Fallon

It bothered her how misunderstood she felt. How people, loved ones, friends, and yes, even fiancés didn't get it, didn't get her. She sat in the coffee shop just across the street from the high-walled cemetery. The day was overcast and cloudy — a perfect day for pictures. Her watch read just after ten. The office had been open for about an hour. She phoned in sick at work today. A weary sigh traveled up to somewhere around her throat. It was no secret that she had no business begging off work. She actually held several jobs, and it was her morning work as a receptionist in Dr. Clarence Marchand's pediatrician office that she called in sick for. Later in the afternoon would bring her position at the department store at the Mall, which stretched into the evening. Then, on the weekends, there was the post at the circulation desk of the public library, and of course, there were also her classes. She took night classes several times a week, working toward a business degree — too much on her plate for a single woman of thirty-five with a bad marriage under her belt. Too much, particularly since her passion these days was photography.

She'd noted the gates of Lafayette Cemetery being unchained only moments before by a thin elderly man. Distracted, she wondered who worked in a cemetery and thought to herself cryptically, perhaps she should, given her pension for eclectic employment.

"Perhaps you should pick one track and stick with it."

That would be Peter, Peter Reynolds, and her fiancé of just under two weeks now. He was a doctor that she'd met when he'd come to fill in for old Dr. Marchand one week. That was the first job, the one she was allegedly sick for today. Peter was younger than she was by nearly four years, which kept her from going out with him at first. It was one of those invisible lines she'd established at some indefinable point in her life. But then, he was particularly persistent, and after a while, another line was broken.

One of the things she liked most about him was that he was nothing like her first husband, except, of course, when he made statements like that.

"You sound just like Jack."

"Sorry, didn't mean to."

25

Peter was quick to be sorry. And that was helpful, but she questioned marrying him. And she questioned picking one track for her life, and mostly she questioned the odd restlessness within her that lately seemed to have become a permanent fixture.

Finishing her cup of coffee, she pulled on the lightweight cotton shirt she'd brought to wear over her sleeveless sweater, just in case it turned out to be chilly this morning. It was late October, almost Halloween in New Orleans, so that made the weather wholly unpredictable.

The streets around the cemetery were largely unoccupied. It was a Thursday morning, and this was not her section of town. This was the Garden District, a lovely area of the city that drew her more often than she liked to admit. What made it distinctive was its texture, its antiquated feel, and its removed aura that tended to convince one it belonged in another place — perhaps another time, wholly separate from anything around it. She'd toyed with the idea of asking Peter if they could move here once they were married. After all, what he would make as a pediatrician would far eclipse what she was managing to live on now. Of course, that would mean she would have to go through with the marriage. She was many things but not a gold-digger, not a mercenary. Marriage would have to be real, for love, not convenience, if it happens at all.

Her black leather boots clicked hard on the cement pavement as she rounded the corner of the old cemetery.

A breeze blew lightly through her thick blonde hair just as she walked beyond the iron gates that led inside. It was as one would expect and yet not. High trees stretched over tall, granite mausoleums, some in perfect condition while others damaged, weather and time-worn as expected. Leaves crackled, and distantly she smelled the dying embers of a fire. Nervously fingering the small camera case around her neck, she attempted to clear her mind and concentrate. Pictures, pictures, she thought if she could sell some to a local magazine then finally, she might be on the right track.

"Perhaps you should pick one track and stick with it."

"You sound like Jack."

"Was that his name? I thought you said, Thomas."

She'd laughed, "No, no you must be mistaken. It was Jack."

Then he looked at her with eyes that said he wasn't so sure but still reassured. "Sorry, didn't mean to."

Her feet wandered through their own volition. She'd been here before but never inside. In her ten years in the city, she'd never wanted to come inside before, until now — until this morning after the dreams, dreams of smoke, bitterness in her throat, smells that burned her nostrils like acid. And then she'd awoken, knowing that she must see inside, not wanting, but needing.

The long blue jean skirt she wore was straight and now felt confining. She should have worn pants, but she hadn't. The skirt stopped her from taking the long strides she was driven to. Surrounding her, the crypts were large — large, tall, rectangular slabs of stone. They were so similar in construction, but the epithets were different: the 1800s, early 1900s, children, families — a child struck down by yellow fever. She took out the camera and began to take shots, shots everywhere, scattered, trees, tombs, broken slabs of stone — just randomly shooting, her fingers quaking as she soaked it all in.

What was it?

She looked up from behind the lens. Elusive but powerful, a pull—it bothered her. Worse than that, it was pushing her, stalking her.

She began to move rapidly but randomly down the uneven pathways between the tombs, reading the inscriptions, looking, feeling, and needing frantically something, something that was here. Her hands reached out strangely, desperately, her fingertips brushing lightly across the etched words, forgotten names.

This pointless action stretched on and on for endless minutes. That was until a feeling of foolishness nearly compelled her to stop. But then lightly skimming across a name delicately engraved on a cold, hard slab of rock, she hesitated, then jolted once it was absorbed.

Impossible, she whispered to herself, staring dumbfounded at what she saw. Again and again, she scraped her fingers along the letters —again and again in disbelief, until her brain soaked in what she saw. It was a coincidence, of course, a name a common name, but hers, her name: "Emma Fallon, Died October 20, 1900."

"Emma, you just called him Jack. His name was Thomas."

She nodded, her mind, or rather her memory, hazy. Then she murmured, "Thomas Woolery."

Peter was looking at her oddly as though she was making no sense, none whatsoever. "Woolery? But your name—"

"Of course," the fog was beginning to clear now. It must be those pills he'd prescribed for her to help her sleep, to help her

sleep dreamless sleep. "I went back to my maiden name. Why would I keep his?"

"Of course," he cut her off. His flat expression told her that he was satisfied. He did have a pragmatic mind, a physician's mind. Things had to make sense to him. "And Jack?"

She rubbed her temples, trying desperately to clear out the cobwebs. "It was his middle name, Jackson. Sometimes I called him Jack." She didn't know why she'd lied. It probably wasn't at all necessary. But the truth, the truth, would have been less palatable to her young fiancé. She had to make allowances for him. He was young in so many ways. The world to him was what he could touch, see under a microscope, and could be explained. To her, it was something different, filled with half chances, mist, incomplete tasks, fractures — not so certain, not so tangible, and not at all as controllable as he would have liked to think. She didn't know who Jack was. It wasn't her ex-husband's middle name. It wasn't a name she was even particularly comfortable uttering. And she had no idea why for a few moments, she was convinced otherwise.

A breeze brushed by her, and it seemed to whistle, whistle directly into her ears, causing pain.

There was a distinctive tap, the tap of a boot on the partial cement walkway that ran along the front of the tombs. She closed her eyes, still feeling the pain in her ears, her head, fingertips still connecting to the tomb, the tomb of a woman who bore her name yet died so long ago. And the tapping, light tapping, was only getting closer. She willed her hand to move, to leave its position connecting with the cool granite, but it would not. So, instead, she willed the tapping to pass her by. No doubt it was close, as it had grown distinctly louder. But again, averse to her wishes, it did not. It simply stopped. Somewhere along the infrequently trodden pathway, it had simply stopped.

She forced her eyes open. Vision was blurry and distinctly out of focus — no doubt the breeze, the chapping wind that felt as though it had dropped in temperature, sometime during the last several moments. She breathed in deeply, extending her other hand and grasping the first, forcing it away from the inscription. There was no point now, no pictures today, she told herself. Something had gone awry and nothing more was possible now. She turned on her heel to leave but then stopped abruptly, jolted. Only a few yards away he stood, a figure, a man quietly watching her.

She didn't intend it, but the suddenness, unexpected shock, sent her eyes into direct contact. A man, bearded, fair, her age, perhaps older, in a trench coat standing there. There was no mistake, just watching her directly. She pulled her light shirt around her more closely, dropping her eyes and readying for a quick departure, when his voice abruptly caused her to halt. "I must know before you leave here if you're all right."

Against her volition, the voice sent her eyes upward again meeting his. She realized he'd taken another few steps toward her, and her immediate response was to back away. But there was nowhere to go. Behind her was the cold, hard surface of Emma Fallon's tomb. "I'm fine." There was a perceptible tremor in her voice.

And then he stepped closer, with, she believed, an expression of kindness on his face. She noted for the first time he was wearing a turtleneck sweater and blue jeans beneath the open trench coat. Odd wardrobe — after all, it was only October. October in New Orleans was not especially cold weather by any means. "Are you sure? You look a bit distressed."

"No," and then she shrugged, "that's not unusual. I usually look distressed." Impulsively, she'd decided to diffuse the awkwardness by taking on a bit of a flip tone.

An amused smile spread across his face, and she thought of Peter and how he was much too literal to appreciate such peculiar moments. "Well, if that's true, it is unfortunate. A lovely lady like yourself should not be so often upset." She detected no particular accent, but he did have a specific way of phrasing words that suggested intelligence or perhaps culture.

"I didn't say I was upset, just that I looked so."

He nodded, "No, you didn't say. But it is more than clear that you are." She hadn't realized when he'd taken that final step, the one that brought him directly in front of her. The one that enabled him to quietly reach up and graze her cheek with his fingertips, "So pale," he murmured. "Have you had a fright?"

The sound was loud, loud enough, so perhaps he should have heard her heart hammering, hammering in fear, or hammering in surprise, of which she wasn't at all certain. Details seemed to be becoming blurred. "No, why would you say such a thing?"

And then the smile, a slight smile that traveled up into blue-gray eyes. "Because it is clearly written all over you, all over your lovely face. That something terrible has brushed by you."

She deliberately stepped to the side, since there was no place to escape backward. "I have to be going," she managed to get out.

But the stranger's eyes were no longer on her. They were focused on the tomb that now lay exposed. And to her complete bewilderment, he reached out his hand, almost tenderly brushing the inscription as she had done herself moments before. "Emma Fallon," it came out in a heavy whisper, his deep voice wrapping around the name in an odd way. And then his eyes were on her, not so kind, not so soft, now remarkably piercing. "Have you heard about Emma Fallon?"

She stood there, struck dumb for a moment, staring at him with puzzlement, "Heard?"

And then he nodded, "Oh yes, so many stories about this young woman. As you can see, she died fairly young."

For a split second, her heart slammed in her chest. She'd been so captivated by the name she hadn't considered the dates. "Really?" was all she said, feeling in the moment a strange, inexplicable paralysis creeping into her flesh.

"Oh yes, young, but a busy life. Some say she was a mystic," and then his eyes narrowed as he focused in on her again, "but others not. Others say she was a witch."

She felt his bold stare and suddenly experienced an odd coursing of strength that seemed to gravitate up her spine. She straightened up and frowned at him explicitly, "Really? A witch? With a long nose and a black cauldron?"

And then the stranger smiled again, appreciating, she was quite sure, her sudden burst of spunk. "Well, perhaps not exactly that kind of witch because I have heard she was quite beautiful. No, I think more so the kind of witch that casts spells, charms, perhaps beguilements."

"Sounds lovely," her voice was dry. She wondered in this odd moment exactly what was going on here. Was this strange man trying to flirt with her or planning a mugging? At this bizarre instant, either scenario seemed plausible.

He dropped his hand from the tomb. "I see you're not one for fancifulness."

She folded her arms in front of her, feeling oddly more vulnerable in the wake of that observation. "Well, life doesn't always leave you enough time for fancifulness."

A thoughtful expression crossed his somewhat rugged face. It was odd. She couldn't truly decide if he was handsome or not. There were sharp planes along his cheek bones that defied that description, but there was also an appeal, something dancing at times in his eyes that could only be interpreted as charming. "Pity," he offered, "when life denies you such enjoyments."

Again, she felt taken aback by his words. Truly, if it weren't for his pleasant manner, she would have sworn he was criticizing her. "Well, as I said before, I have to be going."

"Going where?" he asked softly but pointedly.

"Work, I'm late for work," she lied. After all, she had the morning off. She'd called in sick. But the idea of lingering, continuing this very odd conversation, seemed completely intolerable and out of the question.

"I see," he responded again softly. It was odd how the tone of his voice had become so quiet, soothing, almost wrapping around her when he spoke. "Did I tell you how Emma Fallon died?" Again, a breeze blew near them, the temperature dropping perceptively, or perhaps it hadn't. Perhaps it was simply all in her mind. She was now realizing, in this foreboding moment that she shouldn't be here — that all of this was possibly a terrible mistake. She said nothing but took a step backward, feeling her booted leg again brush up against the last resting place of Emma Fallon. "It was an unfortunate end, you see. But many said she deserved her fate. I don't know if that's true.

What do you think? Does anyone really deserve to die, or to die the way she did?"

"I need to leave now," she murmured, leaning against the tomb, the cold hard surface of the tomb.

"Yes, I know," bending in so close to her, she could feel his warm breath. "But first, I'll tell you how she died." His eyes widened, and she could feel their glare like a tangible stab holding her in place. "You see, her husband murdered her." He lifted his hands in the air in front of her, his strong, long, capable hands. And then he continued in a heavy whisper. "He killed her for betraying him with another man. Witch or not, sorceress or not, she couldn't stop him."

Her vision began to blur before her, a swirl, as she felt his hands go lightly around her throat. "As you can well imagine, Emma, he strangled her completely and without hesitation crushed the life out of her." She didn't know if he'd tightened his grip or what caused all reality to spin and then abruptly disappear into blackness.

"You don't talk about him much."

"Who?"

Peter frowned a bit, and again, she questioned the reasons that they were together. It was not the first time that she thought perhaps it was convenience, timing, or weakness. And as a person, she found him, well, to put it nicely, not formidable. Not like, "Your first husband, Thomas Woolery."

It took a moment for her consciousness to absorb that name. It was there, certainly well-placed in her memory, attached to some face that now seemed to be fading with each passing instant. "It was so long ago."

Again, confusion and then suspicion passed across his still-youthful features. "How long?"

She shrugged, "I don't remember exactly, years. I've lived here in the city alone for years."

His brown eyes narrowed, "But you've only been working with Dr. Marchand for a few months. What did you do before that?"

She'd smiled, trying to smooth things as was her strength in this relationship. "Peter, why all these questions? If you had doubts about me, shouldn't you have considered that before we got engaged?"

"Why are you so secretive?" he'd asked.

It bothered her, irritated her, actually, all the probing. She had answers, neat little answers tucked away in a file in her mind somewhere for such occasions, but now it seemed like such an effort to get to them. "Look, I'm just not feeling well, a headache. How about we do this another time?"

And then he nodded, said sorry, and dropped it. Like she knew he would. And a day passed and another with no more inquiries, and then there was this day.

She awoke to dimness, flickering shadows on a white brick wall, and a chill so powerful that it felt as though the season had changed. Her head throbbed as she sat up on the short pink satin settee. A heavy knitted, ecru-colored afghan was tightly wrapped around her.

She glanced about trying to somehow absorb what she was seeing — another chair, small table, bookshelf all light in color, and the fireplace across from her — the only light in the room.

For a moment, she wondered if she was dead. If, indeed, she had been murdered by the stranger in the cemetery, then she dismissed the possibility. It was a nice room, but there had to be more substance to heaven than a pleasant room. "What makes you think you're bound for heaven?"

The voice behind her was startling. She pulled the cover more closely to her, briefly fearing that she'd been kidnapped and that there were more horrors to come. Then, as he rounded the small couch, he commented dryly, "Don't be ridiculous."

Without glancing at her, he crossed to the fireplace, squatting in front of it, stoking the flames. He'd divested himself of the trench coat and pushed up the sleeves of his navy-colored turtleneck. It was a striking shade against his light-colored hair. He turned to her suddenly, shooting her a wry glance. "Are you reading my mind?" she murmured absently.

"Wouldn't be the first time, love," he shot back, returning his attention to the fireplace. Her head began to throb, and her vision swirled a bit. "Concentrate Emma, you must anchor yourself here."

He was now standing in front of the fireplace, poker in his hand, staring at her with a palpable intensity. She straightened up with an unexpected burst of extreme irritation. "What the hell are you talking about?"

And then he smiled, dropping the dark silver poker down to the brick surrounding the fireplace. "That's better. Use your anger. It will help you regain your place."

She flung the blanket off her, standing up. "Are you out of your mind? What does that mean, my place? Who are you?"

He stood before her quietly, moving no closer, with no laughter in his eyes now. Charm all dropped away, rather perfectly unvarnished. "That's a very good question, Emma. Who am I, who indeed?"

Again, the swirl in her head, voices, phantoms, images melting away in the dim firelight. "How do you know my name?"

A slight smile, "Emma? Emma Fallon, same as the woman on the tomb, same as the witch, the sorceress."

She felt shaky again, losing ground as if the breath had just been knocked out of her. "She died young. Her husband murdered her," she rambled, grasping, grasping for anything.

He shrugged, issuing a quick laugh, "Yes, well, I'm sure he would have liked to from time to time. But then again, it wasn't an untroubled road for either of them. You see, they didn't make it easy on each other."

She breathed deeply, again feeling the swirl in her head but trying to ignore it. She picked up the woven afghan from the sofa and wrapped it around her shoulders. "It's cold in here."

He nodded, "Yes, can't be helped. But there is the fire."

A trembling was going on inside her, her mind, her heart, and throughout the layers of memory peeling away. "I need to go home."

"Yes, of course you do, Emma. But what you need to decide is where exactly home is."

She looked up at him with confusion, feeling acutely, not for the first time, but for the first acknowledged time, the feeling of familiarity that accompanied this individual. "I have to go home to Peter."

"Really?" he said with exaggerated emphasis. His face hardened perceptibly at the mention of her young fiancé's name. "Really, Emma? And exactly what sort of life do you think you'll have with young Peter?"

"Uncomplicated." The answer slipped out before there was thought.

And he laughed in response, "Yes, well, that's true enough." And then he moved closer to her. "It would be uncomplicated, but for a woman like you, wouldn't that be—" and then he brushed her cheek lightly with the back of his fingertips. "Dull?" he whispered.

She looked at him squarely, feeling an odd mix of being compelled and irritated at the same time. "Who are you?" she asked directly and with no hesitation this time.

"Time to remember, Emma," he coaxed softly with that voice, that tone, that compelling, soothing intonation, "remember your first husband."

"Thomas," she murmured, feeling mesmerized, "Thomas Woolery."

He sighed with a bit of exasperation. "Thomas Woolery was my tailor." Then, with a steely voice, he commanded, "Remember Emma."

And then, it came with almost an audible crack, although it was all in her mind. There was a deluge, a flood of color, sounds of music, laughter, dresses of satins, and muslins that cascaded across the floor. And him, his eyes, blue-gray colored. "Jack," she expelled in a gasp.

"Good girl."

Then she turned to him with a genuine anger that exploded like a volcano. "You bastard!"

He smiled broadly, laughing, "Ah huh, remembering too much, I see."

She felt the power of who she was course through her body once more and felt more than inclined to slam him with anything she could put her hands on. "How dare you!"

"You said you wanted time apart."

"I meant I wanted to go to the country, not to another century."

"How is the future, my love? Is it a brave new world? Is it that much better without me around?"

She dropped the blanket on the floor and crossed to the fireplace, resting her hand on its walnut-colored mantle. "Simpler, Jack, so much simpler."

He frowned. Evidently, she'd made a direct hit. "And that is so much better?"

She reveled in the freedom that was coursing through her now. How confining it was not to truly be oneself. "Did you miss me at all?" she asked, a little kinder than he deserved.

There was no smile, but the lights had returned, the dancing lights in his eyes. "If I hadn't, I would have left you there. With your young baby doctor."

She smiled, now beginning to feel the slightest degree of validation, "He's a pediatrician, and you're jealous."

"I didn't expect you to take up with the first silly bloke that approached you."

She looked away, "It's your own fault. You made me forget everything and planted all those silly, false memories. I should have known. Couldn't you have made my past a bit more exciting?"

"Then you would have never wanted to come home," he stated flatly.

And she crossed her arms, truly beginning to absorb the enormity of what her dear, loving alchemist of a husband had done. "I didn't say I wanted to." He moved in front of her, slowly placing his hands on either side of her face. "Trying to strangle me again?" she whispered.

"Wouldn't dream of it, dearest. Come home with me. I'm tired of all of this. I need you."

"And?" she waited expectantly.

With emphasis, he capitulated, "I'm sorry. I shouldn't have sent you away. I just wanted or rather hoped it would help you appreciate more what we have."

She looked away, but he gently tilted her face back to him, "That was a nasty touch, the tombstone, Jack," she murmured.

He nodded, "Trying to jolt your memories. I suppose, in hindsight, it was a bit extreme. But be honest, Emma. Do you really prefer the future?"

She shook her head reluctantly, "No, not really. It's a lot of work. But at least I had the vote there."

He smiled with genuine appreciation, "Yes, well, give it time."

Her husband pulled her closely into a warm embrace, and she knew that this time the wild swirl around them would be the one that took them home.

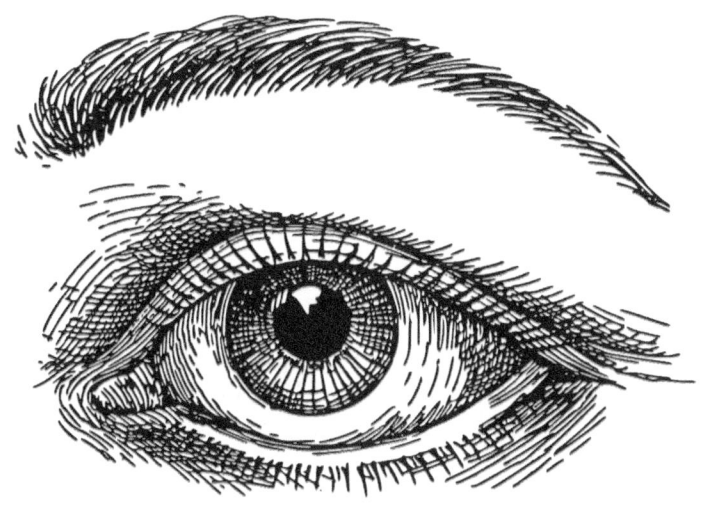

The Soul Shredder

"Is the light bothering you?"

He had dimmed the lights in anticipation of her visit, but she silently shook her head in negation, staring out his office window into the waning illumination of the November evening. He settled behind his desk, waiting for his last appointment of the day to speak to him. Oddly enough, it was a new patient referred by an ophthalmologist — some sort of odd reaction to cornea surgery. Evidently, he wanted to rule out psychological ramifications.

"Quite frankly, Randall, this is a shot in the dark. I've no idea what's going on here. I've done all the tests I can, and the eyes seem healthy, unusually resilient after the surgery. So, all this junk she's seeing, I can't account for it. It goes beyond floaters or adjustment or anything I've seen or read about."

"So, you think it's in her mind."

There was silence on the other end of the phone. But Randall waited. If he was anything, he was patient. It was a tool of the trade. He heard an exasperated sigh, a strange reaction from a physician. Then again, he'd met more than a few who were enamored of their ability and couldn't fathom a problem eclipsing their talents. He did not suffer from such grand illusions. Time and life had shown him quite a different world. And then, after a protracted silence, his friend relented, "I don't know. I can't call this one. She has a peculiar history — bad eyesight all her life until now. Maybe it was too much for her. I don't know. Just see what you think."

And so, the appointment was made and canceled twice. That conversation had been nearly a month ago. But this evening, last appointment of the day, she finally showed up.

Randall Callahan leaned back in his large, dark brown leather chair and tried to stretch out his neck a bit. It ached from the tension that he carried there. He glanced at the clock, 6:05. His receptionist had already left for the day, pleading personal obligations. She rarely, as a matter of course, stuck around past five-thirty. It had been only for the last three months that he'd begun scheduling later appointments. His divorce was final, his house empty. There was nothing to go home to. So, he might as well allow the night to stretch on. He cleared his throat to gain her attention. She still stood by the window overlooking Poydras Street below. His office was on the twelfth floor of one of the taller buildings in the area. But she didn't move an inch in response. She just remained standing with her back to him. "Do your eyes still bother you from the surgery, Ms. Wilshire?"

"No," her voice was soft, nearly imperceptible.

"Well, is it the light here? Is it too strong for you?" She turned around to face him slowly, her face still masked by the pair of oversized oval sunglasses she wore. She was a slight woman, perhaps 5'4", 5'5" at most, with a slight build, definitely on the thin side, with shoulder-length blonde hair. Her face was hard to determine, given the glasses. She seemed attractive, he thought, but it was difficult to assess without seeing the eyes. He'd always thought the eyes were the most telling part of a person's appearance and personality. "Dr. Lariviera said that you complained of some light sensitivity. That is why you continue to wear the sunglasses. I did dim the lights in here in anticipation of your coming."

"Does he think I'm having a breakdown?" she asked somewhat sedately.

Randall straightened up, struck by the directness of the question. "Did he say that to you?"

"No, he did not. I suspect that would have been a tad bit blunt for him. He's not a very honest man."

"Why would you say that, Ms. Wilshire, or can I call you Lila?"

She shrugged, "It's my impression. He tells you what you want to hear, and then," she paused, as if trying to collect her thoughts, "and then makes arrangements behind your back."

"You mean consulting me."

She nodded, "I wonder how many ophthalmologist's patients end up in a psychiatrist's office."

"Well," he laughed, "perhaps those who have adjusting to do."

"He thinks I have adjusting to do?"

"Well, what do you think, Lila? Has your life changed since the operation on your corneas?"

"Changed?" she emphasized the word oddly. "Well, I suppose that's one way of putting it."

He lightly strummed his fingers on his desk. "How would you put it?"

He thought she'd smiled but couldn't be sure. The damn glasses, she would be so much easier to read if he could only see her eyes. "Dr. Callahan, is it? Or can I call you Randall?"

He shrugged noncommittally, caught by her repetition of his earlier statement. "If you're more comfortable doing so."

Unexpectedly, she drifted closer to his desk. And he felt an impulsive chill transverse his spine. But she stopped, oddly right on the heels of that sensation. "What exactly did Dr. Lariviera say to you, Randall?"

"Well, he said you've experienced some odd vision anomalies since the procedure. He told me you'd lived a long time with extremely bad sight, but the advances in laser surgeries allowed him to correct most of your problems. But there have been—"

And she interrupted, "Adjustment problems?" cutting him off directly.

"Is that the case?"

"If they were ordinary, I don't imagine I'd be here."

He shifted in his seat and rubbed his bearded chin for a moment as in some sort of contemplation. It would buy him time and hopefully put her off somewhat. Her directness he found disconcerting. "He did say they were outside his area of expertise. He wanted to eliminate any other possibilities."

"Psychological ones?"

He paused, deciding to refocus things, "Does the light bother your eyes, Lila?"

"Why?"

He swallowed, "I'd like to see your eyes. I connect more easily with a patient if—" His voice faltered as he understood how odd his request must sound.

"I'm tired."

"Would you like to sit down?"

"You don't understand. I'm tired of covering up, of lying. It's using me up, Randall." Her statement he found surprising. Her voice was so flat, devoid of emotion. It didn't match this eloquent plea for help.

"You don't have to lie here, Lila."

She shook her head in negation, "I only told him a little, Dr. Lariviera, just a little bit. And he smiled and told me it was all right, and then I ended up here. If I tell you, where will I end up?"

"I can't help you, Lila, if you don't tell me what's happening."

She stared down at the floor for a moment. And he waited, wondering if this was leading anywhere and feeling inexplicably unsettled by the whole business. But then, she raised her head again to face him. "It's not the light that bothers my eyes."

"It's not?" he asked.

"No, it's just that the glasses keep me from seeing them."

He drew a breath, trying to process what she'd said, "Seeing what exactly?"

Her hands both lifted simultaneously. And as she placed her hands on either side of the sunglass frames, he could see they were trembling, shaking nearly uncontrollably. She slowly pulled the sunglasses off her face and pulled them down so he could finally see her. And in this most peculiar moment that he could only describe as surreal, almost shocking, he wasn't sure if he was looking at something exquisite or something bordering on hideous. They were blue, the eyes, but pale blue like a faded sky or something that had been shielded from the sun all its life. He stifled a gasp. But then the eyes widened and looked beyond him, suddenly examining every space in the room. "I suppose they are from all the different people who come here," she whispered huskily. "They carry them and leave them about."

He followed her gaze and glanced about, seeing nothing but his office as he had always seen it. "What are you talking about, them?"

She wrapped her arms tightly around her, looking a bit stricken but still not focusing on him, just somewhere else beyond. "It's my eyes, you see. He corrected everything too much. I see too much now."

"So, Randall, you met with our strange case last night, Lila Wilshire."

He checked his watch. It wasn't even nine o'clock yet. He was just walking into the building, a cup of coffee he'd picked up on the way still clutched in his hands. He'd have to speak to

Carla, his receptionist, about giving out his personal cell phone number. "I'm actually just getting to my office, George. How about I give you a call later?"

"Look, I'm not looking for anything in-depth, just an impression. Is she off the deep end?"

He paused in the lobby, scooping a morning paper from the security desk. "It's a little early for all that."

The voice at the other end sounded oddly rattled, something he found perplexing. But then again, yesterday's appointment had left him in a similar frame. "Is that it?"

"I just don't want to make a premature diagnosis. I'm sure you can understand that."

"So, you'll be seeing her again."

"Yes, today, in about an hour."

He was nervous. Last night's appointment with Lila Wilshire had fallen somewhere in that gray area between unnerving and downright bizarre. His formal training as a psychologist should have immediately categorized her as a disturbed personality, fraught with extreme bouts of depression and hallucinogenic episodes. That is, if it had been anyone else, that would be his prognosis. But somehow, somewhere, she'd struck a deep chord within him that quite clearly told him she was credible. His intercom beeped, with Carla announcing, "Ms. Wilshire is here."

Uncharacteristically, his heart picked up its beat. He was a bit surprised. Given her initial reticence in seeing him, he had half expected her not to come today, even though he'd strongly urged her to do so.

"It's essential we explore these visions of yours, Lila."

"Why," she'd asked quite flatly. "Do you think you can make them stop, Randall? Do you really think that's in your power?"

He answered the intercom, "Tell her to come in, please." Quite quickly, the door to his office opened as he stood up from his desk.

Again, she noiselessly entered, wearing the same nearly oversized pair of sunglasses. She was dressed in a fitted light blue suit, an outfit that would be striking if not for the odd eyewear. He smiled, determined in the bright light of day to get on a proper footing, a place devoid of so many shadows as the evening before. "How did you sleep?" was his greeting.

She shrugged, "My sleep hasn't been good since the operation. I consider myself lucky if I get a few hours."

"Really?" he sat down as she sat in a chair on the other side of his desk. "That's not good. I could prescribe you something for sleep."

"I don't know," she murmured. "I like to be aware." But she didn't elaborate.

He picked up a ballpoint pen from his desk. He realized dimly that it had been a present from his wife — an impulse gift last year, or had it been the year before? "Aware of what, Lila?" he asked simply.

She leaned back in the leather chair facing him and smiled, he thought. "You remember, Randall? We talked about it last night."

He absently spun the pen around on his mahogany desk, "You talked about them, things you see."

"And you didn't believe me." He glanced up. She was still, eyes focused on him, or as much as he could tell behind the sunglasses.

"That's not true."

"It's not?"

"I didn't disbelieve you."

She laughed unexpectedly. It was a harsher laugh than he expected — not soft like the exterior but brittle like twisted metal. "Now, that's not the same as believing. I bet your wife had fits with you committing to anything."

His eyes widened, trying to digest what he'd heard. "What did you say?"

"I said I bet your wife has fits with you committing. You equivocate."

"That's not what you said. You said you had fits — past tense."

She tilted her head a bit in surprise, "Did I? Well, you aren't wearing a wedding ring. That would make it past tense, would it not?"

"What makes you think I was married at all?"

Then her head straightened, "Last night when I looked at you. It was obvious. I could see it."

"See it?" he echoed.

"When I took off the glasses, I could simply see it. I can't really tell you what, but I could see."

"Take them off now and tell me what you see."

She shook her head. "It exhausts me. I don't want to."

"Are you afraid of seeing them, whatever it was you saw last night?"

"I'm tired Randall, not afraid but tired. Do you see the difference? Whatever is there is simply there."

"Take them off. I want to know what you see," he compelled.

She hesitated, "You want to know. I thought all of this was for me."

He cleared his throat, "I can't help you if I don't know what you're seeing."

And then he detected another smile, "You do equivocate, Randall."

Quite calmly, sharply in contrast to the drama of the night before, she reached up and took off the glasses as if it were the most natural thing in the world. Again, he was struck by the unearthly shade of her eyes, but in the morning clarity, they seemed more normal, not quite so startling. She stared at him directly, quite calmly, not looking about her frantically as before.

"What's changed, Lila? Last night, all of this seemed quite disturbing to you."

She shrugged, looking at him serenely and yet coldly. "I don't know. I think I've given up."

He leaned in, struck by her words. "Given up? What does that mean?"

"I've decided not to fight what is, not to try to change it, not to try to make the world what I want it to be. I've stopped fighting it all."

"So, then you aren't seeing them today?"

Her cold eyes warmed ever so slightly. "I am."

"Now?"

"Now." She repeated.

He glanced around. "Can you describe it to me?"

She nodded rather blankly. "Your room here is infested with different things. Some fly, some crawl. Most are smallish, no bigger than the size of my extended hand."

He smiled, and then a chill flew over him that seemed to support her assertion. "And what do you think these things are?"

Her pale blue eyes widened. "I think they're parasites."

"Parasites of what?"

"Of living, Randall, that's all I've been able to put together. They come. They live off of us."

"All of us?"

She frowned, with a look of fatigue marking her features. "I don't know exactly. I've noticed people with problems, who are weak in some way seem to have more. I suppose they're more vulnerable."

He shook his head, "Problems? What do you mean, sick?"

"Not always, emotional problems. I think they have something to do with energy fields. But sometimes they just come in great hordes and attack no matter what."

He was listening but glanced down at the hand gripping his pen more tightly than he realized. It was disturbing to him, this conversation, more than he cared to admit. "When you say attack, Lila, what does that mean?"

She glanced away toward the window she'd spent so much time staring out last night. "I'm not really sure, Randall. Just that they feed somehow from us, take something, because they get stronger." He sat back, thinking momentarily, unsure where to take this. "You're trying to decide whether to believe me. You know it doesn't matter if you do or not."

"Where do you think these things come from, Lila?" was his next question, and he was unwilling yet to deal with what she'd just said.

"I don't think they come from anywhere, really. I think they're just here, and now I can see them," and then she swallowed hesitantly, "them and—"

He followed the direction of her eyes, which seemed to be on the wall directly behind him. He looked, but again, there was only an emptiness. Then, he turned back to her, "And what?"

"I'm not sure," she whispered. "But I was worried about it. I came into your reception area last week and saw it. That's why I canceled. But then I was worried—" she was almost stammering, nearly unable to put into words what she was trying to express.

"Worried about?" he asked, feeling an odd panic surfacing in his stomach.

And then the eyes, unearthly pure blue eyes, looked at him and seemed to pierce him on some level. "There's a real problem, Randall, a real problem here. It's following you, I think, shadowing you — a thing, a dark thing hunting something."

Her words struck him as fantasy suddenly, nonsensical. "What are you talking about, Lila?"

"I'm not sure. I'm not sure, but I think it's a soul shredder."

Momentarily, a stillness seemed to engulf them. "What did you say?" he asked, reasonably assured that he couldn't have heard correctly.

And then her voice came to him in a whisper, yet it felt like an odd discordant shout inside his head. "I said it's a soul shredder."

His eyes widened as her initial response was reaffirmed. As the cold hand of detached reason finally reached inside him and shook him soundly, he concluded the only reasonable assumption now available from his vast pool of professional experience. The woman was clearly entirely out of her mind.

The wind chapped her face as she walked away from the tall skyscraper that housed the office of Dr. Randall Callahan. It was a bright November day, so she was not out of place wearing her overly large sunglasses. But eventually, night would come and then so would the odd stares, but that was something she could bear more easily than the alternative. She took one last glance back at the building she had exited merely moments before.

A sinking feeling of disappointment tangled around her insides. She'd misread him completely, the doctor. Initially, he'd seemed to have a greater capacity for awareness than nearly anyone she'd come into contact with in a very long time. It was less that she knew this than she felt it — felt it as strongly as she had felt the shroud of disenchantment that he wore like a kingly cloak. She'd always been able to read people long before she could see through them, as she did now.

She headed into the parking garage where she'd parked her car. Her head throbbed from that morning's session. She imagined that fear had gotten a hold of him. That was why he'd stopped listening to her and started greeting her with the psychological doubletalk of a well-seasoned professional, the demeanor of one who had already dismissed their patient. It was remarkably disheartening to her. Oddly, in a very short time, she'd come to like the doctor. He wasn't at all what one would call conventionally handsome, but instead, someone who was well-worn, already a face showing signs of age, wrinkles around his dark brown eyes, but a warmth there, of course, a shrewdness as well. The profession, she imagined, left one jaded.

And it was all a shame because she hadn't intended to see him at all, not until she'd seen it near him.

She reached the darkened second level and walked to her small beige sedan. Her hand hesitated near the handle. Guilt swept through her. She shouldn't have done that — left him alone with it. It didn't make sense, no sense at all. Why him? Why him?

His 10:30 had canceled. So, he could wait until after lunch for his next appointment or go out. But he couldn't seem to drag himself out of his chair. It bothered him immensely, more than he could say —— her story, her long winding story, and then his reaction to it.

"So, this — what did you call it?"

She smiled in that odd, removed way of hers, "Soul shredder."

"Why do you call it that?"

Then, a shadow had passed over her translucent blue eyes. "It's very complicated."

"How so? Isn't this something you've only seen since the procedure with Dr. Lariviera?"

There was a definitive, prolonged hesitation, and he had concluded that in this self-created fantasy she was weaving, it took time to extrapolate the details. So, he was placating and gave her the space she needed to weave. "Actually, I remember it from before, maybe not this one, but one like it."

"Before?" he questioned.

"Yes," she nodded. "You see, my eyes weren't always bad. When I was little, they were quite clear."

"Little, how little?"

"I don't know, seven, maybe eight. Sometime after that, I got sick, very sick, with a high fever. That was when my eyes were damaged."

He nodded, beginning loosely to understand where this was leading. "So, this thing, soul shredder, you believe you saw it before, back then."

Steadily, her gaze took him, and he felt keenly as though she was seeing right past him, past all those hidden places that even esteemed psychiatry doctors kept locked away. "I did see it, Randall. The others, all the other things I didn't, but this one I remember clearly."

He swallowed on a bone-dry throat. It was beginning to annoy him how much all of this affected him. "Under what circumstances?"

The pale blue eyes were steady on him, but she was considering, he thought — considering whether to continue at all. Perhaps he had finally reached the secret core of all of this nonsense. And he would find something he could make sense of. "I would see one, like this one, but not completely the same, around my uncle."

"Your uncle?"

She nodded, "Yes, he stayed with us one summer. We lived in the country. I remember clearly that summer. And it would be around him, at first once and awhile, then more, then always."

He waited for her to elaborate, but she didn't. She just sat in stillness before him, waiting for more questions, more prodding from him. Returning from that distant place of memory, she focused entirely on him. "Are you all right, Dr. Callahan?"

He had to smile. It wasn't Randall as before. Now, it was Dr. Callahan. And he wondered quite distortedly why he deserved that title. He pulled himself tightly back into his role. "Why? Lila, why do you think it—" And then his voice faded off, unsure what he wanted to know. Why was it around him?

Her voice was soft but deliberate. "I can't be sure. I think I know, to feed. It fed off him. I would see it sometimes, doing that."

"See it, how?"

Her face seemed strained at the question, as though recollecting it was painful. And then he mentally corrected himself. It wasn't a recollection. After all, he had decided she was weaving. "I saw it a lot before he left," her voice was nearly trembling as she spoke. "With its hand, it would reach right into his chest, pull something out, and eat it. I know how bizarre it sounds, but it would."

"What did it pull out? Was it blood, tissue? What did you see, Lila?" he asked, with an uncanny need to know.

"It pulled out light. It pulled the light out of him and then ate it." His head pounded at the vision she had evoked in his mind. "I don't know how I knew, but I did even then. I knew it was his soul. It was slowly eating his soul."

He nodded, feeling an odd nausea boiling up inside him, "Soul shredder."

She shrugged, "Just a designation, but it stuck with me all these years."

"Was there anyone else?"

Her face seemed to blanche a bit. "What?"

"Was there anyone else that this thing attacked besides your uncle?"

"No, I—I never saw it. But there were other people around."

"Well, what made him unique?" Question marked her face. "Why him, Lila, and no one else?" She glanced away, not answering, and he was sure she knew. And just as sure that she must tell him before she left his office. "It's important, especially if you're seeing one around here."

"But you don't believe me." Her voice was distant.

"You must have some idea why."

She sighed wearily, a sound that seemed to come from deep inside, "Yes, I suppose. I think it hunts certain kinds of people."

He nodded encouragingly, "What kind?" His voice sounded a bit hard to him given the circumstances, but there was the gnawing need inside him now to understand, to understand everything.

"People, I think, who've made themselves vulnerable."

"Vulnerable?"

"Yes," her eyes had wandered to that window again, where she had spent so much time the night before. He could see now that it was a kind of refuge for her.

"How did your uncle make himself vulnerable, Lila?"

"I think he damaged himself, his soul maybe. He did things that, well, must have marked him some way."

He breathed in deeply as the picture began to solidify in his mind. Her voice was so vulnerable now, so young. He'd heard that tone before, so familiar in victims, very young ones. And then, he asked the question that made the picture complete. "Did your uncle, did he do things to you, Lila?"

Her eyes turned on him, the blue translucent eyes, on him now, hard and biting. "Did he molest me? Are you asking that?"

"Yes," he asked coolly, "is that how he marked himself for this thing to feed on?"

Their eyes clashed in the moment. And he knew, he had his answer, and now a straightforward solution to this self-concocted delusion she had presented him with. "Yes, I think so, Randall. But that doesn't make it any less the truth, the fact that he hurt me. It doesn't make it any the less true that one of those things is standing behind you right at this moment."

He waited, feeling a distinctive chill pass over him. But he brushed it aside deliberately. "It is helpful for a child's mind to concoct ways to lessen their pain, even creatures that might take on the role of the avenger, punisher, for them."

She smiled grimly, "You really believe I've made this up."

"No," he said quite coldly. "I believe your uncle molested you. The rest, I'm quite sure, is a fantasy."

She stood up, a marked expression of disappointment marring her exquisite face. "What about the one I see near you? Aren't you at all concerned that I might be right?"

"Have you seen it reach into my chest and pull out pieces of my soul?" he asked flatly.

She stared at him for a moment, then beyond him, finally shaking her head. "No, no, I haven't."

He stood up, feeling quite justified in his growing disdain for the woman before him. "Well, fantasy or not, Lila, I can assure you I've never molested anyone nor plan to."

She looked at him a little sadly, a little beaten as though some battle somewhere had been lost. "There are other ways to mark yourself, Randall. Please be careful. It wouldn't be here for no reason at all." Then, picking up her purse from where she had left it on the floor, she turned away. Not looking back, but instead putting on her sunglasses, she opened the door and left.

The encounter had been incredibly draining for him. He considered having Carla call Lila Wilshire to schedule another appointment but then thought the better of it.

As he sat behind his mahogany desk, Randall Callahan considered things carefully. He considered his life and his anger and mostly carefully rethought his plans to murder his ex-wife.

Regardless of what he would do, he believed Lila Wilshire and knew that the soul shredder was only waiting for his next move.

Wildflowers

It was an old house — a house in need of repair, renovation, and, as Carl had said, perhaps just a good leveling. And most of the time, she agreed with him. But she stayed on. It had been her Great Aunt's house, left to her completely — an old farm homestead in Virginia. Periodically, there were cows on the adjoining pastures, but they belonged to someone else. She was paid a stipend for the use of her land or, rather, her aunt's land.

Carl couldn't understand how she could leave her high-paying job in Richmond to live in a house once owned by a spinster aunt. "It's madness, Alicia," he had told her. "And I can't guarantee how often I'll be there to see you. I'm booked up with a lot of trips that I hoped you'd be accompanying me on." And she'd just smiled and said it was something she felt driven to do. She needed to get away and drop out of the pressure for a while.

Initially, he had helped her set up the office in one of the spare bedrooms. It was intricate with all the necessary computer equipment. She was banking on eeking out an existence from freelance computer graphics work. And it had succeeded over the two months she had lived in the house. Though ultimately, Carl had been right, his visits had become increasingly infrequent. It was unspoken, but they both knew they were on a downslide. It was only a matter of time. She even suspected he had already met someone. There was no evidence, just an instinct. And it didn't bother her, although it should have. They had been together for over three years now. But the deterioration was gradual, and other things were pulling her — things that were difficult to explain.

She pulled up the window shade in her office. She could see the moon shining luminously from out of the winter sky. It was a crescent, and one brilliant star hung beneath it like a jewel. She had never seen skies like this in Richmond, only here, only now.

"How are you tonight?"

The voice was rich and deep, and although it had startled her, she relaxed almost immediately. Without turning around, she responded, "I didn't realize you were here."

"I'm sorry. I didn't mean to startle you, but it is a beautiful sky."

She smiled, "And you know what I'm thinking too."

"It isn't hard to imagine."

She slowly turned around in the black leather, swivel chair that Carl had given her as a birthday present several years earlier. He had insisted that it was a necessity. Alicia had appreciated it, but the gift had lacked a certain amount of sentiment. "Nice chair."

"And you're sure you can't read my mind."

He smiled, and even though he still stood mainly in the shadows, she could see the brilliant whiteness of his teeth contrasted against the sharp planes of his dark complexion. He walked closer. He wore the familiar wheat-colored cotton shirt and pants and the beaded turquoise necklace that was always around his neck. She remembered the first time she'd seen it. It had immediately struck her as ceremonial, something she would connect with the American Indians. "It was given to me by my father in a rite of passage."

"Would you stop doing that?" she said softly. It should unnerve her, but just his presence had a tranquilizing effect. "Let's just converse the normal way."

He sat on a long cypress bench she'd situated against one of the walls. Like many pieces of furniture in the house, it had been her aunt's. "If you like Alicia," he responded.

He was beautiful. She didn't usually think that of a man, but no other description came to mind, from the smooth, angular dimensions of his face to his warm, dark brown eyes. Even his movements were mesmerizing and fluid, the quiet, smooth grace of his perfectly muscular body. This man was undeniably beautiful. His eyes looked at her with unflinching calm. He didn't know what she was thinking. She had asked him to stop, and he had done so.

"You know the only way to really appreciate the winter sky is to sleep beneath it."

"You mean outside?" she said with surprise, "It's a little cold for that in January, don't you think?"

"Well, if it's not snowing on you, it presents little difficulty," he stated matter-of-factly.

She smiled again, enjoying the odd disconnection of the moment. It was best not to think too much. It would only intrude. "Yes, well, I'll keep that in mind."

"Your aunt did, you know."

Her eyes widened, "Aunt Cathy? That's hard to imagine. She always seemed so meek to me."

He shook his head, "She was a strong, vibrant woman."

"Really? When I knew her, she seemed so reserved."

"By that time, she had already suffered the greatest loss of her life. The man she loved had died, tragically, very young."

It was a surprise to her. Her spinster aunt. Perhaps she'd always been too involved with her own life to consider that the kind old woman might have such a past. "She was in love?"

"Yes, as a young woman and when he died, well, it nearly destroyed her."

"I never knew that."

He spoke calmly and with little emotion. "It was a private thing to her. She wanted me to tell you because she felt as though you might understand."

"Me? Why I've never—" and then she stopped. She always seemed to tell him things that she didn't want to.

"You've never been in love." He finished her thought. "What about Carl?"

She breathed in deeply. She didn't want to think of him now, not here. "Well, I think that's over."

"As it should be, the two of you are too different."

She looked at him with a bit of surprise. "You think so?"

"You don't like my saying?"

"My aunt?"

A fleeting expression of acknowledgment briefly passed over his serene features, but he graciously allowed her to change the subject. "Yes, well, she felt a great kinship with you. That is why she left you this house. So, you could find yourself."

"I didn't realize I was so lost."

Again, the smile, "Didn't you?"

"Did you ever speak to her?"

"No, Alicia," he said quietly, "there has been only you."

She pulled the blanket more tightly around her. She was sick, a cold probably, but she knew there was fever. She had no idea how high it was. That was one thing she hadn't bothered to bring from Richmond — a thermometer. She had been living alone for so long that it didn't seem a necessity. There was no one to ask, "How much temperature are you running?" Luckily, what she did have was plenty of aspirin and soup. Although, in truth, she didn't feel like eating at all. All she wanted to do was sleep, and she might as well because it was snowing outside. It was the first real snow they'd had this winter. She wished that she'd had the energy to build a fire. It would have been wonderful just now. That was the last coherent thought before she closed her eyes.

It was a restless slumber filled with strange, fevered images.

She was outside the house, walking outside, but it wasn't cold anymore. It was spring. And everything around her was blooming in abundance. Her focus was drawn to the figure of a young woman walking in the huge expanse of the field near the house. Wildflowers in soft, vibrant colors were everywhere. The woman wore a hat, a soft straw hat, and a plain cotton dress, light blue. And it occurred to her how her aunt had so often worn that color. In an instant, she had somehow shifted positions and could see the face — a young, beautiful face surrounded by thick dark hair. But there was no doubt who it was. It was a younger, more animated version of Aunt Cathy.

How extraordinary. Was this really what she looked like as a young girl? She was lovely, but more than that, she was so vibrant and happy. And then she saw the tall young man walking toward her in a military uniform. And as her young arms outstretched, there was the smile, the brilliant, dazzling smile that she had never seen before. What does it feel like to smile like that?

Her eyes opened to the soft light of flickering flames. He was kneeling before the fireplace, stoking a fire that hadn't been there before. "I thought this room needed some warming."

She closed her eyes again, "I've been wanting to ask you something."

"What is that?"

"I was wondering if your presence here means I'm losing my mind."

His laughter was deep, warm, and comforting like everything about him, "Do you really think you're losing your mind, Alicia?"

"Well, you have to admit there aren't many options open to me."

"So, I am a product of your insanity." She opened her eyes again. She felt a little dizzy. The fever must have gone up some. "I made you a cup of chamomile tea. You should drink it. It will make you feel better."

She picked up the mug that sat on a chair beside the couch and brought it to her lips. It was sweetened with honey. She hated honey. "It's good for you." She wrinkled her nose at him but continued to sip it. Where did he get honey from? She sure as hell didn't buy it.

"It's hard to just peg you as a delusion when you keep doing all these physical things like building a fire and making me tea."

He came to her and sat on the edge of the couch, gently placing the back of his hand on her forehead. "You're very warm. You don't take good care of yourself."

"You sound like my Mom."

"Your mother is a lovely lady."

"She's dead."

"No, she's a spirit, and we've had many long conversations."

She straightened up a little, unsure how seriously to entertain what he'd just said. "Oh really? About how I don't take care of myself?"

He looked amused. How nice, she amused her delusion, "About how proud she is of you and how worried also."

"And let me guess, she sent you to check up on me."

"No one sent me. I came because I wanted to."

The dizziness seemed to swirl around her, "You do realize you can't be real. You don't fit at all into what my life is about."

"Your life is changing."

Carl was agitated. Of this, there was no doubt. They had met in the small college town, which was, in fact, about twenty miles away from her home. She'd arranged the rendezvous at a coffee house just off campus. It was one Alicia had stumbled upon during one of her infrequent trips to the University library. She'd felt a need to learn more about the area where her aunt's house was situated, about its history. In fact, since she'd moved to her Aunt Cathy's house, she'd been pursued by many unexpected inclinations.

Carl hadn't spoken much since his arrival, just fidgeted with distractions, complaining about administrative headaches at work. She had known him for just under four years. She knew the signs. It was clear he was building up to something.

She looked out the glass picture window, watching the young college students walking by and talking with animation. They still thought that their ideas were fresh and unique, and the world was still a place that could be changed by just the right person. College had been such a haven for her. Stepping out into the real world of the bottom line had been so difficult. It pummeled and twisted those innocent idealists who weren't prepared for its harsh realities. In many ways, it had been devastating, but it had forced her to grow up. But she had to admit, in moments like these, the idea of turning back the clock was appealing, although she would not choose to live through it all again. She could simply not afford the emotional investment.

"What are you thinking about, Alicia? You're so subdued."

"Just reminiscing," she offered unconvincingly.

He ran his hand through his thinning dark hair. "I don't like looking back."

"I know that about you, Carl. So, are you going to tell me the big news?"

He looked up suspiciously. "What news?"

"Well, you seem very nervous about something."

He shrugged uncomfortably. "I'm worried about you, Alicia. I don't like you so isolated, living out in that place alone. You look, I don't know, maybe thinner."

"I've been sick," she said quietly.

"Are you all right now?"

"Yes, it wasn't serious. I'm fine — more reflective, I suppose, though." It occurred to her, sadly in that moment, all the things she'd like to share with him, and all the things she knew he would never understand.

"I'm sorry. I haven't been there to see you more often. It's just—" And then he stopped himself. She sipped her coffee. It was cruel in a way. She had no doubt about what he was about to say. There was someone else. It was written all over his guilty face. And the sad thing was that she just didn't care. Being away from him hadn't strengthened her feelings for him. In fact, every emotion had just sort of fizzled out. Nothing grand just faded away unnoticeably. She truly didn't want to see him suffer. What, indeed, was the point in all that?

She cleared her throat to simulate difficulty, "I wanted to tell you, Carl. I don't know how to say this, but the truth is I have met someone — a man."

He leaned back in the chair, actually looking stunned, as though she had just slapped him. "You have?"

She shouldn't feel such satisfaction at his expression, but she did. It was so ironic that he'd sit up and take notice when she had one foot out the door. "Yes, I thought it's only fair to tell you that he has become very important to me."

"You never mentioned anything like this before. How long?"

It was irritating. He was playing the injured party too adroitly. Perhaps she had made it too easy on him. "I met him shortly after I moved in," she continued. "We became friends, and it's just recently the feelings have deepened."

He looked away from her, seeming genuinely disturbed. Given his recent apathy toward her, it was an odd reaction, maybe a bit unexpected. He turned back toward her, having evidently gathered his thoughts. "I have to say I am truly surprised, Alicia."

She took a quick breath, suddenly not feeling quite so generous. "And what did you want to talk to me about, Carl?"

For a second, he looked startled, his eyes widening for a moment. Then, he shook his head, looking down, "Nothing, nothing of consequence."

"Can you tell me at least who you are?"

"In time," he answered.

"Should I be afraid? I might be too stupid to be afraid."

"You aren't stupid, and there is nothing to fear."

The sun blazed hot all around them. She knew it was the end for him as the guards led the fallen hero toward captivity. But she couldn't reach him, couldn't yell to him, because she wasn't really there. If only he wouldn't fight, but his dark eyes focused on the guard house ahead of him, and he began pulling away from the two soldiers holding him. He thrashed against them violently, yelling, screaming defiance in his native tongue. And she saw the sun reflect off the bayonet before the soldier plunged it into his chest. The agony ripped through her, but then it stopped, and peace flooded everywhere. This was what he wanted, to die with honor.

She awoke in the darkness of her bedroom. Alicia touched her face and felt its wetness, the tears streaming down. He stood near the door, watching her.

"What is this?" she asked.

"Another lifetime, it is of no consequence."

"How can you say that? That was you being killed."

"Go back to sleep, Alicia." He said soothingly, "I promise your dreams will be much calmer now."

The handwriting was her aunt's. She was sure of it. They had often corresponded when she was a teenager, and Alicia spent several summers with her at this house. Her Aunt Cathy had been encouraged by Alicia's father to move to Richmond and let the place go — to be closer to family. But Aunt Cathy had been immovable, adamant, and doggedly attached to her old family homestead. She still had friends in the area and some distant cousins back then who, now, like her aunt, were no longer living.

Alicia flipped through the pages of the old journal tentatively. She'd found it somewhat hidden behind some boxes in the bedroom closet. Part of her felt it was an invasion of privacy. But something stronger was driving her, something that was compelled to know, to try and understand. She was in search of answers, in desperation to find them for herself.

It was dated February 16, 2005. That was the last entry. Alicia realized it was literally only weeks before her death:

It's been days since I've left the house. There does not seem to be a reason. I know I need to go to the grocery, but I just can't seem to make myself. All I need is here. Am I fooling myself? I look into the glass and don't see the old, withered face I had grown accustomed to anymore. It's as though I'm twenty again. Maybe I am losing my mind. But it doesn't feel bad or wrong.

The journal continued,

Every night, he comes to me, Samuel, looking just as he did before he went to the war. Before he'd been killed. Every night, he comes here, and I fix him a wonderful dinner, though I haven't been shopping. I know my cupboard is bare. But there is always something there for me to fix. I like to cook, and I'm not too tired to anymore.

Then afterward, we dance to music, old records from before the war that I played as a teenager. I play them on a phonograph that has been broken for at least fifteen years. But now it isn't. Now it plays. I asked him once what was happening, but he just laughed and kissed me. We don't talk about it now. It doesn't seem to matter.

The other day, he took me out, out of the house to a pretty little chapel near Eastbrook. I wore a lovely white dress that I hadn't seen before. My mother helped me get ready. She and her sister were waiting for us there. She smiled. She was so happy. The church was filled with happy faces, old friends, and relatives. I forgot until just now that most of them were already gone. It just didn't seem to matter. Samuel and I got married that day.

He's not here right now. But I know he'll be back. He's begun to talk to me about leaving this place, my house. It doesn't bother me anymore like it used to. He says it won't be long. I don't think I'll be writing again. Everything around me is different now, and I don't feel interested in how things were before. All the happiness that I ever wanted is here now. I don't want to question why. I don't care. I hear him down the hall. He's back. God has truly blessed me and given me another chance.

It was the last entry in her journal. Alicia's hand brushed over the date. It was less than two weeks later that a neighbor had found Catherine Branton's body in the house. She was in her bed as though she had just peacefully gone to sleep and never awoken.

She breathed deeply. Her chest hurt. As she closed the book, she could feel herself trembling. What did this mean? If she were anyone else who had just picked up her aunt's journal, she would say that its author was old and had slipped into some kind of Alzheimer's or blissful senility. That was a clean, comfortable explanation. But here she was, a relatively young woman, just in her mid-thirties, experiencing something not so very different.

The difference between them was that her aunt wasn't afraid, but she was. Alicia could feel the acceptance tugging at her, the feeling seeping into her that she didn't want to leave this place. Just wanted to let go and drift into whatever was happening. Was she losing her mind? Was she going to be found here dead in the house one morning — that is, if anyone bothered to check up on her? And how much did she care? Did she really care at all?

She sat in her aunt's bedroom, in her bedroom now, in the great four-poster rosewood bed that virtually filled the room. It was covered by her aunt's hand-made quilt and lots of pillows. Those Alicia had added.

The heavy white plastic, hand-held mirror she clasped in her hands had been in a drawer in one of Aunt Cathy's dressers. Although its surface needed a good cleaning, the reflection clearly stared back at her.

The image wasn't a young woman of twenty. Her face was already beginning to crease, the wear of life, a few strands of gray twining through her thick dark hair. It was her as she had always been. She wasn't seeing any deception. The eyes were just as wide and brown, and the face was somewhat strained and pinched from her recent weight loss. Who had said that? Carl? Hadn't he said she'd lost weight? There wasn't a scale here. And she had no friends to tell her that it was so. There had only been Carl, and he was gone now. She was alone, isolated.

It had been weeks since she'd talked to her brother in Boston. He'd left a message on the answering machine, but she hadn't called back.

That was different for her. It wasn't like her to ignore obligations. She was a detail person. She had prided herself on that at work. But all the tidy threads of her life seemed to be drifting off somewhere, unraveling.

Was she like her aunt?

Would she be creating a new life here built on her own insanity?

What was happening? The walls of the old house seemed to whisper it back to her. What was happening?

"I need some answers."

He looked at her from across the den, his dark eyes calm, unreadable. "I know you do."

"You know, I don't even have a name for you."

"You used to call me Joseph."

"When did I call you that?"

"When we met, many lifetimes ago."

She shifted restlessly on the couch, her head pounding. "What do you mean? You mean reincarnation?"

He walked closer, stopping in front of where she sat on her aunt's moss-green-colored sofa. He knelt before her and lightly brushed her face with his hand. It made her tremble, although his skin was warm, real, not a ghost. It was flesh. "The answers are difficult, Alicia."

"So are the questions, Joseph." She pronounced his name with a deliberate irritation, but he just smiled. "Tell me, how did I know you?"

"We were not together in life. I met you on a vision quest."

"A what?"

"A vision quest, an altered state — a journey of the spirit that young men of my tribe would pursue. I sought spiritual knowledge and—"

"And you met me?"

"You were my guide."

The breath caught in her throat as she tried to absorb what he was saying. "You're serious."

"I told you the answers would be difficult." He paused for a moment as though choosing his words carefully. "You called me Joseph because when we would be together, that would be my name. You were my teacher then," he gently clasped her hand. "You looked different. Your hair was long and blond." And then he smiled, "The color of honey. But the eyes were always the same, brown filled with humor, as though most often things struck you as funny. And you always came to me garbed in a long flowing robe in the color of a lush green forest because it was my favorite color. When that life ended, you were the one who met me and led me forward."

"But you're here now."

"Yes," he said calmly, his dark eyes fixed on her intently.

The question hung in the air between them for a moment before she found the courage to speak it. "Does that mean I'm getting ready to die?"

He touched her hair softly with his hand, "I don't know."

"I think it's time for me to leave here," her voice shook. "I'm not going down without a fight."

"You always fight Alicia, even what you know to be true. I've watched you struggle with truths all your life. Acceptance is something you must learn."

"Don't you know what this seems like to me? How impossible all of it is?"

"Perhaps that is the point, Alicia — to stretch the boundaries of what you consider possible."

She breathed in sharply. "Did my aunt lose her mind?"

"No, not the way you are thinking. She breached the confines of this life's reality. She spent some time here between before she crossed over."

"Crossed over to what? To death?" She shook her head. Tears were running down her face, "I don't understand."

He softly stroked her cheek, "No, you do understand. You just resist what is true." Then he leaned forward softly and kissed her. His lips were warm and real, like his skin.

She was breathing deeply but was calmer. He mesmerized her, making her forget the confusion — lulling her into acceptance. She whispered, "Are you sure you aren't some kind of vampire sucking away my will to live?"

He laughed softly, "I'm sure, Alicia. I'm an old friend who came to spend time with you." It felt familiar and comforting as he pulled her close into his arms and held her tightly.

The hotel in Richmond felt cold to her, not warm and comfortable like her aunt's house. But she had driven all night to get here.

It was about two in the morning when she'd woken up. Joseph was not beside her. She'd felt chilled throughout as a panic had overtaken her. She didn't know why, but it had. She'd woken up afraid — the slimmest thread of self-preservation pushing her to go, to go now quickly before he came back to make her forget who she was.

She packed a small bag—not all of her things, just essentials—and fled into the night, driving away from the mystical place of complaisance.

It was about five o'clock now. She had checked in several hours earlier, not being terribly selective about where she stayed. At this point, it was too exhausting to care. There was plenty of time for changes in the morning, but so far, she hadn't been able to sleep. Her head throbbed with pain. There were decisions that had to be made. Would she sell the old place? She could, and it would finance a move up North, closer to her brother in Boston. It would be a new beginning. She could find a new job. But she'd have to close up the old place with her aunt's things.

Her eyes were so heavy. If she could sleep for a little while, she could figure everything out. She wondered if she should call Carl but then remembered distractedly that he was seeing someone else. She didn't really want to see him anyway. She just wanted to fill up her time with things, mundane things to do — just to fill up her time.

The weather was warm, and everything was springtime around her. Wildflowers, purple and soft yellow, rippled gently in a quiet breeze. She walked along the field that led down toward a lake. There was nothing but trees and nature everywhere. It was blissful serenity, as a dream should be. She sat down on the shores and stared up into a sky of the purest blue.

"I like this place."

She looked up at Joseph standing beside her. He wasn't smiling, just watching her tentatively. He sat down beside her and pulled a long, thin weed out of the ground that he absently twisted between his fingers.

"You know. You didn't have to run off in the dead of night. I wasn't holding you there."

She turned to him, "Weren't you?"

He sighed, "You are always doing things like this, you know, impetuous."

"That's what you like about me."

"You know. We are going to be together."

She leaned back on the grass. It was peaceful now. "I know, but not yet, I have things to finish."

He nodded, "Yes, it seems you do, beloved."

She laughed. "I like that, beloved."

He took her hand in his, and the dream went on for a bit longer.

The Left Palm

F ear, a manifestation of fear, certainly this was it. It was the only explanation, the one that made any sense she could live with.

She looked outside the bedroom window of her apartment onto her small, secluded concrete patio. Hopefully, this time, it would be gone. Shakily peering through the blinds, her heart clutched in her chest. It was nearly midnight, but the nearby streetlamps still illuminated the enclosed space, reflecting off its thick black coat. It turned its face toward her, unmistakably a pure, black wolf with eerily pale blue eyes.

She stepped back, allowing the blinds to snap back into place.

Again, it feverishly crossed her mind to call the police, the SPCA, or the fire department — frankly, anyone. But each time she moved to pick up her cell phone, a paralysis crept in. Something inside her refused, absolutely refused to follow through.

She silently crept back onto her daybed, pulling the covers around her. In the morning, it would be gone. It always was. After all, this was the third night in a row she'd seen it.

It was summertime, unbearably hot and humid in the city. But she made her way to the college by the lake, where she was taking one graduate course in Victorian Literature. It was a nine o'clock class. After lunch, she would head to the French Quarter for the rest of the day, where she worked oddly enough as a Tarot card reader at a small shop on Chartres Street.

Granted, it was an odd profession, but it was one that she literally fell into. She'd been working at a gift shop on Decatur Street and, feeling the pinch of inflation, began looking for a second job. There was a sign boldly taped on the door of *The Left Palm* — "*Looking for Part-Time Help.*" Seeing it, she just sort of drifted in with no idea of what she was getting into. The front of the store was filled with books, candles, and even clothing, so quite naturally, she'd assumed it must be a sales position.

The lady who greeted her from behind a glass counter was older, at least in her late fifties. She had long black hair, dramatically streaked with gray, piled up in a low bun behind her head. Quite a striking image. She wore an electric blue caftan dress and an ornate oriental scarf draped across her shoulder. But when she'd met her eyes there was no smile, rather an almost suspicious expression reflected through her intently plucked dark eyebrows. "Yes," she'd asked nearly sternly.

She breathed in deeply, suddenly feeling as though she'd like to slink off somewhere and forget the whole thing. "Well," she hesitated, quelling a bizarre combination of panic and curiosity, "I saw your sign outside about a job opening."

The slim, dark woman leaning over the glass counter in front of her now straightened up. It was difficult not to be struck by the regalness of her bearing. "You're looking for a job?" she asked flatly.

"Yes, I am."

"It's part-time."

She nodded, feeling amazingly uncomfortable, "Yes, that's fine."

And then she outstretched one of her hands, ornamented by very long, bright red nails, and placed it flatly on the glass case in front of her. "So, you're a reader."

She hesitated, "A reader?" asking with surprise.

"Yes, we need a Tarot reader." Suddenly, Claudia glanced around the store and took it all in — crystal balls and new-age paraphernalia. Of course, now she understood. It wasn't a sales position at all. Again, the woman repeated in low tones, "You are a reader."

And Claudia with great confidence met her dark eyes and answered quite directly, "Yes, I am."

Actually, before working at *The Left Palm,* it had all been a hobby, an eccentric interest. She'd done Tarot readings since high school for friends and relatives, but never herself. Long ago, she'd recognized that she simply couldn't read for herself. It was too personal; rather, she was always searching for something. And it was frustrating because more than she wanted to know anything, she wanted to understand about herself. She needed to know why all her romantic entanglements ended disastrously, if she'd ever finally finish her degree, if she'd stop having to work so much, and if her life would ever settle down. But *The Left Palm* had proved more lucrative than she had imagined at first. The pay was largely commission, and before long, she had developed a clientele. At times, she'd found the work less than rewarding and, at its worst, completely draining.

Fortunately, and unfortunately, the money was too good to relinquish. Even with an assistantship at school, there were too many bills to pay. So, Claudia continued to read people's fortunes, all kinds of people.

And on the early morning drive to school in late July, she wondered if there was some connection in this, in her work and the black wolf that had prowled her patio for the last three nights.

It had rained earlier in the morning, which increased the humidity to an almost stifling extent. She'd always loved this city but did not love the summers. She yearned for the fall again, when it would be easier to breathe.

As she entered the English building, hearing her sandals lightly tap on the stone floor, it struck her suddenly how deserted everything seemed. Granted, the summers were quiet here, but this morning seemed exceptionally hushed. When she'd arrived, she'd noted a few souls wandering about in the parking lot and then sitting on the steps of the library as she passed by, but the English building was now virtually empty.

Then, as she finally reached the classroom door, she understood at least one of the reasons why: A note, "*Class Cancelled*." She thought longingly of how she could still be in bed catching up from another largely sleepless night.

Her thought was to go home and try to catch just a few more hours, but such fatigue suddenly filled her that she couldn't even muster the effort. So, instead, she wandered outside and sat down on the first bench that came along. Just a few minutes, she thought, only a few to regroup. She leaned against its wooden frame and closed her eyes, trying to draw energy from anywhere.

It took some moments before her eyes flickered open again before she noticed that a rather substantial shadow had fallen over her. But when she did, she instinctively straightened up in a jolt. It was quite unexpected. Not a cloud passing over, but a man standing in front of her—a man dressed in a black suit, a few feet away, just watching.

The sun shone directly in her eyes. With one hand, she blocked the glare, trying to get a clearer glimpse of this stranger. Bearded, dark, possibly black hair, but fair skin. She straightened up a bit more, expecting something from him, some sort of conversation, but nothing.

"Umm, can I help you with something?" she asked in puzzlement. And then, an unnerving wide smile spread across his face. Suddenly, a flash of sunlight stung her eyes so painfully that she quickly squinted. But more disturbing was that when she reopened them, the stranger was gone. She bolted up, scanning in all directions but seeing no one remotely resembling his form. He'd simply vanished. An unexpected chill of fear traveled up her spine and spread out, making her skin feel like ice. She quickly began heading back to her car, moving so fast that it nearly felt like a run.

"You look awful."

After an hour of sleep and a quick shower, she had somehow managed to drag herself into work for noon. Madame Christina stood behind the front counter with a frown on her face. Over the years Claudia worked at *The Left Palm*, she'd come to a plateau of understanding with the shop owner. Christina Duverje rarely smiled, had a sour disposition, and was profoundly psychic. Once you accept all these facts about the woman, life working at the French Quarter shop could be bearable. "No sleep," she murmured as she crossed the threshold. "Any appointments today?" she asked, secretly hoping there were none. Between the wolf literally at her door and the disappearing stranger at the University, her nerves were frayed to the point of unraveling. What would be most medicinal would be a nice, quiet, uneventful afternoon.

"No, my sweet," the older woman commented. "Just a few stray walk-ins this morning. Wednesdays, as you know, are notoriously slow around here. But I have some new stock you could put on the shelves while I go to lunch."

Claudia nodded. For a moment, she thought about confiding the recent bizarre occurrences in her life to her boss. But something kept her silent. Somehow, talking about them felt as though it would become more real. Madame Christina had already gathered her things from a locked drawer beneath the counter. "You can ring me on my cell if things get too busy. Marguerite will be in at one. And I probably won't be back for a while. I'm meeting an old friend."

Claudia smiled with distraction as her boss noiselessly exited, except, of course, for the delicate chiming of the bells positioned strategically over the entrance. She breathed out a deep sigh of fatigue. It would be an hour until their very high-energy palmist swept through the door, hopefully, a quiet hour to regroup. She sat on a stool behind the glass counter at *The Left Palm* and attempted to clear her mind. She felt stress all over her, crawling over her skin, sapping her strength. She should have simply called in sick, but the truth of the matter was she didn't want to go home. The memory of the black wolf prowling her patio last night left a fear wrapped around her heart. It was clear that whatever was happening couldn't continue. She needed help, but exactly what kind of help was the ultimate question.

Claudia was deeply lost in thought when the bells at the doorway of *The Left Palm* chimed to signal the entrance of someone. She came to her feet quickly but, in the next moment, stood literally rooted to the spot as a man rounded the corner of a book display. Her breath caught. There was no mistake, the black suit, pale face, and now, as he approached the counter, she could clearly see the ice-blue eyes.

He stood before her, not unlike he had done earlier at the University. But there was no hint of expression on his face, just a calm appraisal. They stared at each other silently, and then, almost against her will, the words slipped out, "What do you want?"

Now, there was a smile, the kind that didn't touch the eyes. He spoke in a low voice with a clipped British accent. "Why, I think I'd like a Tarot card reading."

They were like booths, partitioned with long red curtains at the back of the store. Madame Christina had set up the first one with a slim sightline through the curtain to the front entrance. Business wasn't booming enough that there would always be more than one person working at a time. So, this was a way to alert a reader if another person was in the store. Within each booth was a card table covered by a soft white, silken scarf and two chairs on either side. They were actually nice, padded armchairs that Christina had obtained from a friend at a nearby antique store. It was all very atmospheric, which was necessary, given that they charged sixty dollars for only a thirty-minute reading.

And today, Claudia was giving that reading to a man who called himself simply "Neil."

She had no idea why she was doing this. It was crazy. It was crazy. A thousand excuses, a thousand lies had flooded up to her mind the moment he asked for a reading. But she seemed incapable of uttering even one, just stood there staring at him blankly, as though he had just asked to clean out their cash register. And then he'd further inquired quite placidly, "Is that all right?"

And she answered too quickly on its heels, "Yes," without paying attention to what her brain was screaming at her. The man himself was calm and collected and showed no indication whatsoever that he'd ever laid eyes on her his whole life. And then, the doubts crept in. Perhaps it was her. Perhaps she'd had some premonition of their meeting. That was why she'd seen him before. But why and what did it mean?

And here she was only moments earlier feeling content and pleased to have the shop to herself, and now literally counting down the minutes until Marguerite flew in the front door like a tornado. Blessed tornado, for once in your life, please be on time.

"Is everything all right?" he asked.

She glanced up at him, again entertaining the gaze of those strange, blue eyes. She'd tried to avoid looking at them too often. They were pale, disturbingly pale. She had tried to somewhat gauge the man's age but found it difficult — late thirties, early forties, hard to say. And that suit was one of the oddest things of all. It was a nice suit but so unsuitable for this time of year — so heavy, so hot. Then again, maybe he worked in a funeral parlor. She started to shuffle the oversized Tarot deck in her hands and leaned back in her chair. "No, everything's fine. Have you had your cards read before?" she asked, her eyes still downcast, concentrating on the shuffling.

"How old are you?" She looked up, a bit surprised at the question.

"I'm twenty-four," she answered guardedly.

He nodded, "Seems young."

She stopped shuffling and, perhaps a bit too abruptly, placed the cards on the table. "If you'd prefer a more seasoned reader, Madame Marguerite will be back in this afternoon."

"No," he murmured. "That's not what I meant. And yes."

She looked at him with puzzlement, "Yes?"

"You asked if I have had my cards read before."

She looked down again, nervously picking up the deck. "Oh yes, well, is there anything in particular you'd like to know about?"

Again, he answered "Yes" rather quietly.

She glanced up. He was watching her with that odd curious expression as though he was expecting something. "Well, as you shuffle the cards, you should concentrate on it."

She reached over handing him the deck and feeling the brush of his fingertips as he did. The contact was startling and disturbing. The only way she could describe it was electric and cold at the same time. She pulled her hand away, feeling an absolute numbness in her fingers now. Instinctively, she glanced through the slim opening in the curtains toward the front door, but there was nothing, no movement. And then she glanced at her watch, forty minutes until Marguerite. Murmuring to him, she said, "We'll begin now."

She glanced up, noting that he'd stopped shuffling the cards. Suddenly, she realized she'd neglected to pull out a significator. "I'm sorry, I forgot—"

But then she stopped mid-sentence as the man who called himself Neil was holding a card to her. "It's all right," he said. "I pulled it myself."

She hesitantly took the card in her hand and flipped it over. "The Hermit," she read. "That's an unusual choice. I mean for someone whose—"

"Not old?" he finished. She looked up again. He was smiling that slightly odd smile as though he was somewhat amused. "Well, I might be older than you think." And then he handed her the deck.

"You really should cut them three times."

Slowly, he shook his head, "Not necessary. They're fine."

She nodded hesitantly, placing the Hermit in the center of the table as she began the spread.

"You have a strange style."

It was her job interview or, rather, her audition as a Tarot card reader for Madame Christina Duverje. At the time, she'd smiled back at the dour older woman, feeling without question there was no way in hell she was getting this job. She had no professional experience as a Tarot reader, and this woman, well, oozed expertise in so many spheres.

She continued driving home her point, "You're very weak on specifics." She glanced at her over the Tarot spread that Claudia had just boldly read for her. Naturally, she had given her all and hadn't held back. It wouldn't do, she thought, to appear hesitant. After all, she believed these people were seventy-five percent theatrics anyway. But now, her potential, and she used that word shakily at best, boss was glowering at her. Christina Duverje eyed her critically, slowly shredding away any feigned confidence she'd brought with her. "You know," she went on, "Clients like specifics. The man they're going to meet, who will have a baby, illnesses, even who will kick the bucket." She delivered all of this with a straight face, as these were only the facts of the business. And then she pointed one of her menacingly long fingernails at her, "But you, you're too vague."

She nodded, mentally considering what her next plan of action would be. Maybe a job at a mall, although she hated the late hours. And then Madame Christina had completely surprised her. She had reached out with one of her elaborately manicured hands and placed it atop Claudia's. She looked up into the older woman's dark eyes. "But you know, I really think there's something there. With a little coaching, you could do this." She literally couldn't believe what she was hearing. And, good to her word, she had coached her, albeit briefly, just enough to get her up and running. But today, in front of this man, she could feel all of that confidence she'd built up over the past year slowly melting away.

She swallowed on a dry throat as she finished laying the Celtic spread, her hands hesitating over the cards. Again, it was crazy. This not only seldom happened. This never happened. It was all major Arcana cards. The first twenty-two cards of the Tarot, the most powerful cards in the deck, and this guy had ten of them, plus the Hermit that they'd started with. "Umm," she began, just stunned. "Are you sure you shuffled these well?"

"Yes," he answered pointedly, "as did you."

She nodded. That was right. She had shuffled them. And she did see him do so, or at least she thought she did. "This is just very strange."

"Really?" he answered with little emotion.

She glanced up, "Would you like to redo it?"

"No," he stated flatly.

She frowned, "Okay," distractedly, placing the rest of the deck down on the table.

"Do you read palms?" he asked.

She looked up, "No, our palmist will be arriving very soon if—"

"No, I was just wondering if you did."

She forced a smile and shook her head, "No, sorry. No, just the cards."

"I wondered because of the name of your shop — The Left Palm."

"Madame Christina does read palms as well," again seized with the hope that their interaction would be cut short.

"Do you know what that means?"

She stared at him blankly. "I'm sorry?" she said with genuine confusion.

"The Left Palm, do you know its significance?"

She shook her head slowly, "No, not really," feeling that chill sweep over her again, the one she'd felt at his fingertips.

He spoke slowly and deliberately, "The left palm charts the path of the spirit. Did you know that?" he asked with deliberation. Again, she shook her head, feeling greatly unnerved by this turn in the conversation. And then, he placed both hands face down on the table before her. "I'd like to show you something. So, you can get an idea of who I really am." She stared at him, confused but unable to utter a sound like before. Then, slowly, he turned over his left hand, and at that moment, time truly did seem to stop. Her eyes blurred over in disbelief at what she was seeing. His hand, his entire palm, had no creases, no lines in it at all. It was entirely blank.

"Oh God," she finally managed to mutter brokenly.

"So, now Claudia, I would like to spend these last minutes we have together not reading my cards because, as you might have guessed, I know exactly what they say. But instead, having a little talk that is long overdue."

It began when her grandmother died. She'd been ill for some time and had stayed with her family at her parents' home toward the end. She'd even briefly shared a room with Claudia, which had made the little girl, who was only eight, somewhat uneasy. It wasn't the recognition of her grandmother's failing health or even that particular sensation of agitation that seemed to surround the older woman at the end. It was as if her soul was fighting the change. It created a discordant feeling between the body and the spirit that felt the pull to escape. Of course, all of this, she didn't recognize at eight. But she did see them — all around, and in the end, all the time. Some were spirits that looked like a bright glow of light, and others came in more tangible forms, people moving around the room, talking to her grandmother — whispers all the time, whispers, and then, the last night, right at the end, the angels. Beautiful lights, white, gold, long robes glowing, when they took her with them. When her grandmother did pass on, it hadn't registered at all to Claudia that there was still a body there. She had already left with the angels, and a disturbing emptiness remained once they were gone.

She breathed in deeply, deep, painful breaths of fear. "Oh God, what do you want?" she asked.

He smiled coldly, so coldly. "Now, we get down to it. There's no reason to panic."

"The wolf," she whispered.

"A messenger to let you know I was coming. But I see you didn't quite get that, did you?"

She glanced around, looking at the door. Still no sign of Marguerite, and it was ten to one. "She's going to be late," he stated flatly. "Late enough for us to finish this."

"Finish what?" she snapped out.

"I need a promise."

"You're out of your mind. I'm not signing anything." She almost yelled emphatically.

He laughed softly, leaning back in Madame Cristina's antique chair, "You've seen too many movies. No, my dear, you're not important enough for that. I just want a promise."

"What kind of promise?" She knew she shouldn't have asked. She knew she should have run, run like crazy to the nearest holy ground. But instead, she asked what should not have been asked.

"I'm busy."

She stared at him blankly in bewilderment, "What?"

"What I need is less complications."

"And I need a vacation, what's your point?"

He smiled, "Actually, you've hit the nail on the head. You need a vacation, and I need fewer complications. All I ask from you is that you live your life—a nice life, perhaps a comfortable life—but stay out of my way."

She stared at this strange aberration of a person in complete confusion. "What?" was the only response she could think of, "What does that mean?"

His pale face hardened a bit. Evidently, she wasn't giving quite the expected answers. "Let me paint you a picture, my dear. One life — things go smoothly. You finish college. You get a nice job. You get a house and a car. You marry a nice man, have children, and live quietly and peacefully. Sound nice?"

She shrugged. Did he really want an answer?

"Another picture," he continued in a silky low voice. "A life of struggle — it takes a while to finish school, and there is not enough money. It is not so easy to land a job, and things interfere, unfair things. You continue to work, sometimes several jobs. No house, not enough money. Maybe no husband, maybe no children. Always a battle, always some impediment. Sound nice?" he asked with an edge of sarcasm.

"So, you're saying if I stay out of your way, I get the first life. And if I don't?"

"The wolf will always be at the door," and then he smiled coldly. "So, to speak."

Her heart thudded loudly in her chest. Her head was spinning. Was this real or some sort of deluded dream? Impossible, how could it be?

And then the answer came to her softly, almost silently, in a whisper — angels. She remembered now from back then. She'd told her mother about them, expecting, completely expecting her to say she was crazy or that she had imagined them.

"You didn't," she'd said. "It's a gift that you could see them, and they'll always be there for you when you need them."

And she had. She'd seen them again five years later when her mother died unexpectedly. She knew then that she was right. It had been and was now a gift.

For a moment, the coldness seemed to lift enough for her to think clearly. So, she reached out slowly and gathered the cards together quietly, glancing down at her watch. She met his ice-blue eyes and said calmly with confidence, "Your time is up."

He frowned explicitly, "Are you sure you're making the right decision, Claudia?"

She nodded with assurance, "Yes." And kept him in her sight until he left.

Finis

The Lady in the Blue Dress
6 x 9 Softcover & Hardcover 214 pages
ISBN 978-1-61342-600-5
ISBN (Hardcover) 978-1-61342-418-6

When she was a child, Mika Devalieur was introduced to her grandmother's most precious possession — a priceless and mysterious painting that she simply called The Lady in the Blue Dress. Upon Adele St. Clair's death, the painting is left in the care of her granddaughter with only one stipulation. Mika must hand over the family heirloom to a total stranger. Mika Devalieur desperately wants to deny her beloved grandmother's last request, but she can't. Torn between her Gran's last wishes and her desire to hold onto the Lady, she ultimately journeys to rural Virginia, where an enigmatic man shows her that this painting is only the beginning.

What quickly becomes clear is that James Clairmont knows much more about her and the Lady than he is letting on. He begins to slowly unravel a powerful supernatural connection that spans three generations of her family. Mika finds herself desperate to uncover the entire truth before she falls in love with a man filled with so many secrets — secrets about him, about her, and most especially about The Lady in the Blue Dress. (First published on Kindle Vella, episodes 1-23.)

The Tethering
A Portent of Crows
6 x 9 Softcover & Hardcover 201 pages
ISBN 978-1-61342-599-2
ISBN (Hardcover) 978-1-61342-419-3

Deborah Brandt's beloved Aunt Gena always told her that she was special, a bit different, and would have to live her life, unlike other people. Of course, this she disregarded as the ramblings of her lovely but notably eccentric aunt. Although there were the things that Aunt Gena said that seemed true — like Deborah being sensitive to energy shifts, having potentially psychic impressions, and dreaming of a spirit guide — none of it could be real. But the most ridiculous thing that her Aunt Gena told her before she died was that someone special was out there for her. She said that he was an extraordinary man who was not only her perfect match but someone who she would learn from so that they could help the world in difficult times. How ridiculous! It sounds like a fairy tale, and no such person exists.

Daniel Wren is unique. He has been raised and trained from a young age to hone his psychic gifts. He lives in a world unimagined by most. And he has been waiting for years to contact his counterpart, soulmate, if you will. But the problem is that she is painfully unaware of the type of life that he lives and the life she would be entering into if they came together.

His dilemma becomes how best to proceed. How can he win her over and move forward before outside forces take that decision away from him?

Dumaine Street

6 x 9 Softcover & Hardcover 306 pages
ISBN 978-1-61342-902-0
ISBN (Hardcover) 978-1-61342-416-2

Voices in her head, catastrophic emotions, hallucinations — Rebecca Wells is more than convinced that she is losing her mind. And as a last-ditch effort, she contacts a self-professed counselor who seems convinced he can help.

Gabriel Sutton has abandoned the world of medicine to navigate a realm filled with psychic phenomena. Diagnosing Becca with extreme empathic abilities, he struggles to help her stabilize her gifts while trying desperately not to fall in love with his patient.

From the realm of vulnerability into a crusade to use their profound gifts to rescue others from peril on the other side of death, these two follow an astonishing and unpredictable path into each other's hearts.

Travels into the Breach

Accounts of a Reluctant Mystic
6 x 9 Softcover & Hardcover 171 pages
ISBN 978-1-61342-323-3
ISBN (Hardcover) 978-1-61342-417-9

At first glance, his life seems quiet, serene, and even uneventful. Malachi McKellan, a 65-year-old widower and author of esoteric books, lives largely as a recluse in a house situated just off the banks of Bayou St. John in New Orleans. But unbeknownst to most, he is also a bit of a detective, a specific kind of detective whose specialty is psychic attacks. Alongside his lifelong companion and spirit guide Simon Tull, a 19th-century, 20-something English gent, Malachi battles the unseen, and is an unacknowledged hero to the most vulnerable. Most of the population have no idea what is really happening beneath the surface of the world in which they live.

In this collection of adventures, Malachi McKellan and Simon Tull wage war against the most insidious elements of the paranormal. In *The Three*, Malachi and Simon come to the aid of a young woman being victimized by a group of dark witches. An old apartment building is the scene of an unimaginable battle against monstrous forces in *The Lost Soul*. Malachi and Simon find themselves strategizing against a psychic vampire in *Obsession*, and *The Hotel* turns back time to the 1980s where Malachi confronts a demonic spirit. In *Between*, a past life is revisited as Malachi attempts to rescue a beloved sister from committing her existence to vengeance, and *The Wedding* takes a personal turn when Malachi must confront painful truths while endeavoring to protect his niece from a potentially devastating union.

Travel into the breach with a pair of paranormal warriors who choose to confront overwhelming forces on a battlefield unsuspected by most.

Gravier's Bookshop

A New Orleans Paranormal Mystery (#1)
6 x 9 Softcover & Hardcover 172 pages
ISBN 978-1-61342-288-5
ISBN (Hardcover) 978-1-61342-411-7

Max Gravier had no intention of becoming a recluse, but after his wife's death it seems his life is heading in that direction. He spends his time running Gravier's Bookshop on Magazine Street and occasionally on the quiet helps the police solve a crime with his psychic sensitivities. That is until he answers Caroline Breslin's call, a cry for help out of his dreams that draws him into a fierce battle for a young woman's soul.

In this first installment of The New Orleans Paranormal Mystery series, Caroline Breslin, an amazingly gifted empath, is determined to strike out on her own and has moved out from the protection of her family home. All is going extremely well until, of course, she comes under siege from a devastating supernatural attack. The last thing Caroline wants is to run back to her family for help, even though she is painfully in over her head. What she really needs is a knight in shining armor — or maybe just that guy that keeps haunting her dreams.

Join them and the whole Breslin family psychic clan in this first installment of The New Orleans Paranormal Mystery Series where you'll travel into a new world just a few steps into the turbulent realm of the unseen.

The Hotel Mandolin
A New Orleans Paranormal Mystery (#2)
6 x 9 Softcover & Hardcover 146 pages
ISBN 978-1-61342-290-8
ISBN (Hardcover) 978-1-61342-412-4

Peril is wrapped up in the most enticing of disguises in *The Hotel Mandolin*, the second installment of The New Orleans Paranormal Mystery series. It's opulent, classic, and one of the most renowned hotels nestled deep in New Orleans' famous business district, but something is amiss at The Hotel Mandolin.

PI Peter Norfleet is calling out the big guns to help him investigate a recent suicide at the famous establishment — his good friend Max Gravier, a formidable psychic, and his girlfriend, Caroline Breslin, a talented empath. But none of them can seem to scratch the surface of this puzzle, no one except Cassie Breslin, Caroline's clairvoyant mother, who has somehow tapped into an unexpected connection with a tragic ghost from the turn of the century. And the more she uncovers, the more dangerous and malevolent the mystery becomes

The House at Pritchard Place
A New Orleans Paranormal Mystery (#3)
6 x 9 Softcover & Hardcover 138 pages
ISBN 978-1-61342-292-2
ISBN (Hardcover) 978-1-61342-413-1

Nothing is really wrong with the old Warrick House on Dante St. except that there most certainly is. Nothing is exactly wrong with its new mysterious owner except that Elise is sure that something doesn't add up. It isn't obvious, but sometimes the most dangerous things aren't.

In the third installment of The New Orleans Paranormal Mystery series, with the help of her very psychic sister and her children, the Breslin clan, Elise Ashford is about to embark on a wild rescue mission straight into another dimension that will land her squarely somewhere she doesn't expect, right back into her past. She'll land full circle; in a childhood home whose memory still haunts her to this day -- *The House at Pritchard Place.*

Treading on Borrowed Time
6 x 9 Softcover & Hardcover 223 pages
ISBN 978-1-61342-214-4
ISBN (Hardcover) 978-1-61342-436-0

For Julia Moreau, life seems complicated. Emerging from a failed marriage and managing a lifetime of diabetes, she lives alone in her childhood home where she communicates with the spirit of her Great Aunt Lilia. But Julia doesn't have a clue what complicated is until she is thrust into being the key chess piece in a match between two powerful men of extraordinary abilities on the wild hunt for a mystical creature hidden in the heart of New Orleans' French Quarter. Will Julia lose her soul to the karma of a devastating past life or her heart to the love of a man driven by dark forces? What is clear is that whichever way she turns she is *Treading on Borrowed Time.*

Sanctuary of Echoes
6 x 9 Softcover & Hardcover 371 pages
ISBN 978-1-61342-211-3
ISBN (Hardcover) 978-1-61342-409-4

Ghosts unacknowledged do not sleep.

Corey Knight has resigned herself to a quiet, reclusive life spent living out the rest of her days in her childhood home on the fringes of New Orleans' French Quarter. But the unexpected specter of her deceased father plunges her into a mad quest for a missing supernatural weapon unearthed long ago. And unfortunately, her only ally is a lost love she once betrayed.

Iain Shaw returns to New Orleans, a city he abandoned a decade before while fleeing a devastating past. Here, he is forced to confront it again in the visage of the woman he once adored - one that he is now determined to get back at any cost.

Follow them both in a wild paranormal tale of discovery and redemption as they confront and unearth the echoes of a buried and unyielding truth that once tore them irreparably apart.

A Quiet Moment
6 x 9 Softcover & Hardcover 273 pages
ISBN 978-1-61342-326-4
ISBN (Hardcover) 978-1-61342-435-3

Jacob Wyss is caught in a rut, in fact on the verge of being engulfed by it. After an excruciating and disillusioning divorce, his life as an artist in a sleepy-college town at the foot of the Appalachian Mountains has become quiet, routine, and maddening in its predictability. One wintry day, his deep restlessness drives him out in precarious conditions to a largely empty bookstore nearly devoid of another living soul, nearly.

Aimee Marston isn't like everyone else. On the surface, she lives a sedate life working as a feature writer for a small local newspaper in addition to several other editorial jobs to help make ends meet. But just beneath, her existence is largely not her own. She is a sensitive, an empathetic psychic, guided by her calling to use her gifts to help others. Unfortunately, as a result, her secretiveness has made her defensive, protective of herself, and prevented her from having much of a life.

A psychic call for help sends Aimee out on a freezing January morning where her destiny and Jacob's collide sending both their lives spiraling onto an unexpected and often disturbing track. Two lonely souls connect, not by accident, but by design. Theirs is the intersection of two spiritual paths, two lovers who must struggle to overcome the phantoms of a past life, as well as the challenges of their own inner demons to carve out an extraordinary future together.

A Ghost of a Chance
6 x 9 Softcover & Hardcover 230 pages
ISBN 978-1-61342-162-8
ISBN (Hardcover) 978-1-61342-440-7

You never know what's coming next.

Jack Brennan, an ambitious high-powered attorney, dies. But that's not the end, rather only the beginning. He finds himself constrained to an inexplicable afterlife as an earth-bound spirit trapped in an old Virginia farmhouse. His only companion is a very much living, reclusive writer of campy vampire novels. The maddening problem is that Hallie does not know he is there, nor that he is somewhat reluctantly falling in love with her.

Hallie Barkly is recovering from a painful and disillusioning divorce. Out of the ashes of her former life, she has managed to somehow forge a career and exorcise her demons by writing under the pseudonym of Sebastian Winters. Slowly, she is awakening to the fact that she is not alone.

Their lives intersect, and two unconventional lovers are brought together under insurmountable circumstances. Together they must battle an unseen force hell-bent on possessing Hallie's life and bridge death itself to make possible what cannot be — to find a chance.

Dragonflies - Journeys into the Paranormal
6 x 9 Softcover & Hardcover 176 pages
ISBN 978-1-88756-072-6
ISBN (Hardcover) 979-8-32548-418-6

In every form of creation, there is a blueprint for living, for experience, for interpretation. In flight, they can twist, turn, alter direction, pause in midair, and even fly backward. The dragonfly is the master of adaptability. They are a living prism, refracting light, and color, seemingly shifting their essence.

The lesson the dragonfly gives is that life is never what it appears to be.

In "The Wizard," as a novice practitioner of magic, Aurora Finn finds herself battling against the illusions of a powerful wizard intent on separating her from the world she knows. "The

Sojourners" is a gentle story of a mother and daughter whose tenancy in an old Virginia farmhouse uncovers the trials and sorrows of its former occupants. A bookstore clerk gets an extraordinary customer on Halloween night in "Late One Night at Berstrums Books." In "The Tear," a woman coping with her fatal illness unknowingly begins a track on a mystical journey that will entirely restructure her vision of the world.

These stories follow the path of the dragonfly imbued with the momentum and energy of change, taking a winding and treacherous journey that ultimately leads to truth buried beneath perception.

Breaking Through the Pale
6 x 9 Softcover 134 pages
ISBN 978-1-88756-045-0

Journey with metaphysical author Evelyn Klebert into a collection of short stories that travel beyond the pale into the unpredictable realm of the paranormal.

In "A Grey Mourning," a disillusioned man encounters a mysterious being on the foggy streets of New Orleans. "Contact" is a tale of automatic writing, when a young artist establishes communication with a spirit guide, and the victim of a car crash unravels the true nature of her existence in "Dancing on the Threshold." The final tale is called "Isolation," in which a confused and disoriented woman finds herself in an old, quaint house where she must piece together the mystical implications surrounding her predicament.

The Witches' Own
6 x 9 Softcover & Hardcover 140 pages
ISBN 978-1-61342-058-4
ISBN (Hardcover) 978-1-61342-428-5

On the surface things seem quiet and serene in the pictur-esque coastal village of Kilmarnock, Virginia. But something unseen roams its lush forests as the past and present collide and the unthinkable begins to wreak its vengeance. Young Lucy Bonner is executed for witchcraft in the town's distant and bru-tal past. Her death triggers an unholy chain of events which grasp at the restless heart of novelist Peter McQuade, spurring him towards a quest to uncover the dark and terrifying truth.

Appointment with the Unknown
The Hotel Stories
6 x 9 Softcover & Hardcover 155 pages
ISBN 978-1-61342-360-8
ISBN (Hardcover) 978-1-61342-421-6

A hotel, for most, represents a normal place, a predictable realm of commonality. One might even go as far to say a safe space, the reliable where nothing particularly unusual is ex-pected to happen. Or is it? Dimensional traveling, spirit guides, mystical storms, and soul mates separated by time are only a few elements dotting this supernatural landscape. Drop into a collection of romantic paranormal stories where that place of commonality is only the threshold, the jumping-off point, for extraordinary adventures into the unknown.

White Harbor Road

And Other Tales of Paranormal Romance
6 x 9 Softcover & Hardcover 152 pages
ISBN 978-1-61342-066-9
ISBN (Hardcover) 978-1-61342-441-4

A psychic soul mate, a time traveler, a horror writer, and an enigmatic stranger take a selection of resilient, life-battered heroines to a place of paranormal healing and transformation. In this collection of short stories, *White Harbor Road* is the last stop where life's burdens and hardships evolve into something unexpected.

The Broken Vow
Vol. I of The Clandestine Exploits of a Werewolf
6 x 9 Softcover & Hardcover 204 pages
ISBN 978-1-61342-133-8
ISBN (Hardcover) 978-1-61342-420-9

In the heart of every man there is a history. In the heart of every monster there is a story. In this first installment of *The Clandestine Exploits of a Werewolf*, Ethan Garraint is on a vendetta that begins in the heart of the Pyrenees with the fall of Montségur and leads him to the streets of New Orleans nearly five hundred years later. But the person he chases isn't really a man anymore and Ethan has been a werewolf for almost a millennium. With the aid of a gifted seer, he is on a blood hunt that will culminate in a journey that crosses the line between heaven and earth and ends somewhere in between.

Considerations
6 x 9 Softcover 68 pages
ISBN 978-1-88756-062-7

Sometimes the struggle to understand the meaning and complexities of living comes down to a single moment of introspection or a fleeting yet meaningful reflection. This collection of poetry by Evelyn Klebert takes you down a winding path of self-discovery where the resolution may not always be absolute, but the journey is indeed unforgettable. It a wide and varied map of inspired poetry for your examination and consideration.

Explanations
6 x 9 Softcover 82 pages
ISBN 978-1-93493-515-6

In this, her second poetry collection, Evelyn Klebert takes us down the intricate path of a personal journey. Life with its particular struggles, pitfalls, and ultimately triumphs clearly begins to mirror a universal path, the quest for answers that we all ultimately pursue. In this reflective, esoteric collection we can all explore and seek some of life's elemental mysteries and hopefully when all is said and done emerge with some *Explanations*.

Visit Evelyn's website at:
www.evelynklebert.com

Cornerstone Book Publishers
www.cornerstonepublishers.com